# HAVOC FOR SALE

# HAVOC FOR SALE

John Jakes began his career as a writer of mysteries before turning to such historical novels as *North and South* and *California Gold*, upon which his popular reputation rests.

*Havoc for Sale* is the second of four adventures featuring the diminutive private investigator with flaming red hair and a taste for outrageous adventure. In this episode, Johnny is working as a television repo man in the suburbs when trouble finds him in the shape of a beautiful housewife.

Originally published as a paperback by Belmont Books in 1962, this edition, with a new introduction by the author, marks its first appearance in hardcover.

# HAVOC
# FOR SALE

# JOHN JAKES

THE
ARMCHAIR
DETECTIVE
LIBRARY

Originally published by Belmont Books in 1962
as a paperback original entitled
*Johnny Havoc Meets Zelda*
First Armchair Detective Library edition: October 1990
1 3 5 4 2
The Armchair Detective Library
129 West 56th Street
New York, New York 10019–3881

**Cataloging–in–Publication Data**
Jakes, John. 1932–
[Johnny Havoc meets Zelda]
Havoc for sale/John Jakes.—1st Armchair Detective Library ed.
p. cm.
"Originally published by Belmont Books in 1962 as a paperback original
entitled Johnny Havoc meets Zelda"—T.p. verso.
ISBN 0–922890–23–4 (trade) $17.95
0–922890–21–8 (collector) $25
0–922890–22–6 (limited) $75
I. Title
PS3560.A37J66    1990
813'.54—dc20       90–1186

Printed in the United States of America

# HAVOC FOR SALE

# INTRODUCTION

Once upon a time, my quartet of novels about a 5'1" private eye had some pretty good titles. Then the publisher got into the act. . .with, presumably, a better sense of what the market wanted.

Or was it a sense that the books had to be tarted up with misleading titles and cover art because they were too off–the–wall to sell very well on their own? (If that was the answer reached by the editorial wizards at the long–gone Belmont Books, I'm glad they didn't tell me. No, actually, I'm grateful: I wanted the books published, crummy titles or not.)

Publishers aren't entirely to blame for all the trouble over titles. Almost any writer will tell you that a potent title is hard to come by. Such a title should be catchy, and inviting, and suggest the nature and content of the book without giving away one iota of the story. Luckily, I've always had a facility for titles, able to find (most of the time) a pedigreed performer among the dogs. Maybe it's all the hours I spent hunting for the right two or three words in an ad headline for some product or service I was hyping in my suit–and–tie days (I couldn't afford the three–piece jobs currently in fashion with CEO'S and yuppie bond salesmen).

I will say that good titles never come quickly for me, or easily. But the wait, and the struggle, are worth it.

Thus I reacted with predictable pique when this Johnny Havoc novel, the second of the four, appeared under the godawful title *Johnny Havoc Meets Zelda.* I'd sold the manuscript under another title which I thought ideal.

But it wasn't sexy. And in those days (1962), sex was selling paperbacks. Or trying. Thus, inching steadily toward the titillating, the third Havoc novel was re–titled *Johnny Havoc and the Doll Who Had "It."* The fourth and last came out as the leeringly salacious *Making It Big,* which I suppose you could interpret as having something to do with success; but I didn't and I expect the departed moguls of Belmont didn't either.

There was not so much as a by–your–leave regarding these little modifications. Back then I was lumping along as a journeyman paperback writer, and the standard boilerplate contract reserved to the publisher the right to edit or change a title without permission or consultation. Now I've got it in my contracts that my title is my title, period, and if anyone is going to commit another *Making It Big,* it'll be me.

But the panjandrums of Belmont obviously believed they knew better than the poor hick in the provinces, at least for their market, in their day. All I can say is, in their infinite wisdom, they're gone, and as a character says in a great Stephen Sondheim song in *Follies,* I'm still here—thinking up titles.

So now, thanks to Otto Penzler and his new imprint, not only can you read *Havoc for Sale* the way the author wrote it, you can read it the way he titled it, too.

That makes me happy.

Just think of all the threatening letters I don't have to ask my attorney to write.

John Jakes
Greenwich,
Connecticut
June 15, 1990

# HAVOC FOR SALE

# Chapter One

THERE ARE SOME limits past which no hustler should go, even chasing frivolous things like office rent money or dinner at a Nedick's stand once a day. I refer to the city limits. It was pretty shocking to discover you could get lumps in the suburbs just the way you can in seedy city gin mills where the inmates wear the latest by Smith & Wesson; I'd always thought suburban 'ife was one long four-color gate-folded paradise.

Oh, the approach was peaceful enough. I tooled my heap (that was *another* payment overdue) out of the city onto the freeway around five, top down, enjoying the countryside and the bumper-to-bumper exhaust fumes. After about twenty miles I crossed the line into Sylvan County. Before long I curved down a long cement spiral exit ramp. I consulted a map. I was practically on target. I drove around a short curb in the feeder road and came square on a twenty-four-sheet billboard:

Welcome to
## OLYMPUS ACRES
*The Home Buyer's Heaven On Earth*
4-bedroom suburban estates—no cash down!!!

I parked and fished out the collection service work sheets. The particular estate I wanted belonged to a party named Ned Jones. He could, apparently, afford four bedrooms but he'd skipped the last nine payments on his $500 all transistorized Kool Tube Combination Family Fun Center, which is advertising for a television-FM-stereo with cherrywood veneer at extra cost. Noting the address, I started up again, feeling gloomy. That I

5

should be reduced to birddogging for a city collection agency—!

The agency owner was so cheap he wouldn't hire his own leg men, or even a licensed private detective. I'd tried to convince him he should pay extra for a jack-of-all-opportunities like myself, since I was unencumbered by licenses and the like and could therefore do a superior job. He spotted my hungry look and said nuts. I took his first offer, and all the TV time payment contracts he'd bought up. The one for Jones was at the head of the list.

As I cruised along the twisty streets of Olympus Acres I was hit with a gooey feeling that maybe I was making a mistake hotfooting around the greedy city after my livelihood. Look how pleasant it was here. Balmy July twilight —the Fourth was only a couple of days away—drifting through tall trees which the builder, in some moment of mercy, had left unbulldozed. Around the hundreds of houses on the gently rolling hills kids splashed in plastic pools, power mowers coughed and backyard barbecue grilles sent up peaceful smoke signals.

But as I approached the block where I hoped to find my quarry, I smelled a rat.

How could a builder possibly put up homes so big for no cash down? The lots were larger and more secluded than in most of the developments I'd seen around the city. The houses fairly gleamed split level modernity. There were little touches like redwood patio fences and black iron lanterns by the front walk.

I cruised past one joint on a low hillside. The windows were vacant. A *For Sale* sign stood on the crab grass. Where the top soil had been washed away in some rainstorm, I saw a fat black crack in the foundation. The whole port side of the house seemed in danger of sinking.

My confidence in man's cupidity was restored. I pulled up in front of Number 72 Mohawk Trail. Then I did a double take.

The house itself, concealed in a grove of birches, was no bigger or smaller than others around it. The lawns on either side were neatly manicured but the grass at Number 72 was going into weed. Every other drive had its Falcon or its VW, but Number 72 had a long black Imperial crouching in the carport. The neighbors had all their casement windows flung open to catch the breeze but Number 72 was shut up tight.

Well, Jones couldn't fool me. I leaned back against the cushions and lit a smoke. I gawked like a lost tourist or prospective buyer. I noticed that the freeway ramp I'd come down was only two blocks straight ahead—the curving drives of the development twisted back on themselves before you knew it. Across the street from the Jones property was a genuinely deserted house with an *Open House* sign on the lawn. I got out of the car and walked over. A spaniel real estate salesman exploded out the front door and rushed toward me. I turned away fast—and turning, saw the drapes flutter in the Jones living room.

Before the salesman could retract his fingers I was across the street and up the Jones walk and banging on the door.

The number that answered was the kind of suburban matron manufactured only by M-G-M.

"Something I can do for you?"

"I have some papers for your husband, Mrs. Jones."

The dolly frowned vacantly.

"Mrs. Who-did-you-say?"

"Don't stall. I know this is the Ned Jones house. Where is he?"

She smiled down limpidly from her black, fetching eyes. She stood almost six feet, being what they call the Junoesque type. She had rich black hair and a dimpling expression that made it clear there wasn't much upstairs. The lower floors, however, were swell.

Her wrapper came unwrapped as she reached forward to unlatch the aluminum screen. I feasted on a view of astonishing breasts and wished I was eleven inches taller.

"My name's Zelda. What's yours?"

"Havoc, Johnny Havoc. Look here, Mrs. Jones—"

"Cut out that stuff. I told you my name's Zelda."

"I don't care if it's Nefertiti, I have to talk to your husband."

"Husband?" Zelda batted her store eyelashes. "Whom do you mean?"

I slapped the papers with some irritation. "Ned Jones! He owes nine back payments on your combination Family Fun Center."

"No Ned Jones here. I told you my name was—"

"Wait a minute, wait a minute. Aren't you Mrs. Jones?"

"Of course not, silly."

I took a deep breath, settled my porkpie firmly on my head and reached for the screen knob.

"We can settle this inside. There's been a mistake—"

*"No mistake, shrimp. Hustle back to your kiddiecar and don't bother us."*

"Who said that?" I peered around for the source of the male voice.

The body that belonged to it stepped into sight behind Zelda. "I did."

The bruiser glowered at me. He was at least two inches taller than the girl. He had shoulders almost as wide as a sawhorse and piggy brown eyes set in a lumpy face that had taken plenty of knocks. His sneer got my temper going.

"All I want is Ned Jones. Is that you?"

"He's my brother," Zelda said. "His name's Lee Roy."

"Shut up, Zelda."

"Need any help, Lee Roy?" asked a new voice from the living room shadows.

This addition was a wart more my size, an axe-faced young party with straw hair and blue eyes. He wore a gaudy flowered summer shirt and kept working a cigarillo back and forth in his mouth. Zelda framed the words *my brother* as he crowded up to the screen. I wondered who the dumb broad was trying to kid. The three of them looked about as much like relatives as Georgie Jessel and Whistler's Mother. Lee Roy noticed the byplay and gave Zelda a shove in the ribs.

"Go back to the kitchen, stupid."

Zelda shrugged. The wrapper fell open. "Sorry, Mister Hammock." She gave me a long, liquid glance that said she was sorry just because I was a man, and that some time it might be a novelty with a guy my size. Then she vanished.

"You got the wrong house, buddy," Lee Roy told me. "Okay?"

"The hell I have. Number 72 Mohawk—" I stopped.

"What you staring at, creep?" said the number with the cigarillo.

Staring must have been the word, but my ears had picked up the original surprise—a raucous racketing from deep within the house. It sounded exactly like the jack-hammer drills you hear on a construction project.

"Leave me handle this, Doug," said Lee Roy. He put his face close to the screen and scowled unpleasantly. "I'm getting tired of you, shrimp. We don't want no Fuller Brushes, we don't want to be surveyed about teevee, we don't want nothing but you to go away before we have to get rude."

"Oh yeah? I've got a collection to make in this house and I'm going to—"

*Slam.*

I heard the lock click. I let out a sigh. Either Ned Jones had paid thugs for bodyguards or there was something pretty fishy going on inside this outwardly respectable suburban manse.

I walked around the corner of the house. I pretended to start down the driveway. Then I ducked under the carport and around the black Imperial into the backyard. It was overgrown with weeds and crabgrass isolated by a high privet hedge. Inside the patio fence I spotted the kitchen door.

Prudence advised I should get back to my heap and get out. But I've never been known for prudence, especially when people begin to make remarks about my stature. I figure a guy with my build has got to hustle twice as fast as a six footer, just to show the world that short people don't have to take a back seat to the over-sized clowns who run things most of the time.

The minute I opened the kitchen screen, the door whacked open and Lee Roy and Doug crammed through at the same time. They shouldered me back onto the patio and boxed me into a corner of the redwood fence. Beyond the high privet I heard the chatter of people having a cook-out in the next yard.

Lee Roy cracked his knuckles menacingly. Doug rolled his cigarillo back and forth.

"You're askin' for trouble, shrimp," said Lee Roy. "Else you wouldn't nose around after we told you to get out."

Now two more joined the festivities. One was Zelda, appearing in the kitchen. Behind her stood another gent whose puss seemed somehow familiar. He was short, barrel-chested, with thick hairy arms showing below the rolled cuffs of an expensive white shirt stained with gray dust. His round, scarred face looked as though it had been run through a hamburger grinder. Thinning black hair was a good indicator of his forty-five or so years. His eyes reminded me of a lizard in the zoo.

"Who's the punk?" When he talked he curled his upper lip in a cheap imitation of Humphrey Bogart.

"Some collection agency creep hunting for Jones," said Lee Roy.

Zelda pressed the best parts of herself against the screen and tried to smile helpfully. "Look, Mr. Hammock, my brothers don't mean no—any harm. They just don't like to be disturbed. This used to be the Jones house, but it ain't—isn't—no more. Any more."

"I don't have any notice that Jones moved," I told them.

"No Jones here," said Round-face, doing the lip trick. "Better get that through your head. You boys," he said to the phony brothers, "get him off the property. If he acts smart, just remember the neighbors." He shoved

Zelda out of the way and slammed the door. A moment later the muffled racketing began again.

Doug gave his partner a broad wink, indicating he understood I had to be treated carefully since this was a respectable neighborhood. But the set-up itself was hardly respectable. There had been a hardness, a coarse familiarity about Round-face that told me I wasn't playing in the Little League any longer.

"We tried to tell you Jones wasn't here," Lee Roy said. "Now why don't you go check a phone book?"

"The phone book says this is it."

"You got an awful wise tone for a guy who only stands five feet," said Doug.

"Five feet one, pal. And unappreciative of your sarcasm."

Lee Roy licked his lips speculatively. "You a cop?"

"How could he be a cop in that tight suit?" Doug said. "Them Brooks Brothers rigs don't leave a guy room to carry a sack of peanuts, let alone a heater."

"I'm no cop," I said, "but maybe I'll round up some and bring them back to see what gives."

Lee Roy let out a long sigh.

"That's all. Doug, take him from your side."

I unbuttoned the two buttons of my coat and waited, a little cold in the gut but relishing the prospect of getting in at least a few good ones. Laughter came from the barbecue on the other side of the privet. The fun lovers might have been on the Moon for all the help they could give me.

The two uglies closed in with sure, deliberate steps. Doug lifted the aluminum chaise and set it silently aside.

"Forget what you saw around here, shrimp," said Lee Roy. "Else you'll get a permanent dose of what you're gonna get right now."

"The hell I will. I'll—"

Lee Roy's fist in my belly made me cough out the rest of the words. Doug delivered a kick to my privates. While I gasped for air against the fence Lee Roy chopped the side of my neck. I went down to the flags on hands and knees. Everything was spinning.

I shook my head from side to side to make them think I was hurting worse than I was—which was bad enough —and grabbed Doug's brown and white sport shoes. With a curse he fell. I crawled over him and held his chin with my left while I gave him my right full blast. His nose began to bleed.

Lee Roy hauled me off and tried to chop me down. I snatched his wrist and gave him some leverage I learned in Army basic. He flipped through the air and landed on his head. He bounced up instantly.

"Little sonofabitch fights dirty," Lee Roy wiped his arm across his mouth. A red gleam shone in his eyes. He'd crossed the limit of having a job to do and now considered to make it personal. He lunged forward, "I'm gonna make him remember never—"

Doug stepped into his path. "For God's sake, Lee Roy, don't go crazy or the boss—*ulf!*" He caught the punch I'd aimed for his partner.

The pair of them stumbled around a minute, giving me the opportunity to wade in and let Doug have a couple of kidney punches of a kind I'd learned back in the city. He dropped to his knees. I would have finished him, but Lee Roy grabbed a handful of my hair and lifted me off my feet just long enough for one powerhouse right to the midsection.

Bells dinged in my ears. Roman candles went off behind my eyeballs. Lee Roy dropped me on the flagstones like a sack. I tried to struggle up. Both of them had recovered enough to jump on me at once. From there on I never had a chance.

The job was quick, dirty and thorough. A few good stomps in the ribs. A couple of nice twists to the leg. Then they changed places. Lee Roy held me while Doug punched me. My head snapped back and forth like a tennis watcher's. When I went down the last time Lee Roy would have given me the blade of his hand across the Adam's apple if Doug hadn't torn him off.

"Christ, Lee Roy, calm down!" His voice was distant, filtered through a foghorn. "Any more noise and we'll have those jerks in the next yard over here. We can't risk killing—*damn it, Lee Roy, you heard me! Get up!*"

Cursing, Lee Roy tottered to his feet. Flat on my back and aching like hell all over, I could barely focus on the thick finger he pointed at my chest.

"Just remember, shrimp. The next time you ring our doorbell, you won't walk away on legs. They'll carry you in a limo with a big red cross on it."

The back door slammed. The lock snapped. The flagstones began to tilt and whirl under me like surfboard. I closed my eyes for a nice long rest.

# Chapter Two

WHEN I MADE my somewhat painful return to consciousness, the lightning bugs were out and a mosquito was practicing dive maneuvers in the vicinity of my nose. I stood up. The patio floor swung about 45 degrees, then settled back level. I groaned just to prove I was still alive.

Voices were still raised in noisy conversation beyond the hedge but the Jones house (or was it?) showed black from end to end. Close examination revealed that heavy drapes had been pulled, even across the kitchen windows.

I laid my ear against the face brick. Sure enough, the muffled hammer-hammer-hammer was still going strong. That, however, was the only sign of life.

I cat-footed to the Imperial and noted that the goons had left my heap undamaged. I leaned against the black fender and lit a soothing smoke.

Now, Havoc, I said to myself, you have two choices.

One, you can highball it back to the city and get clear of whatever illegal mess is being hatched inside the mysterious house—it's a cinch Zelda, her phony brothers and the oddly familiar round face are not suburban types at all, unless you consider Ossining the suburbs.

Or, two, you can pursue the trail of the elusive Jones a bit further (my merely remarkable sense of profits in hiding was now fully aroused) and maybe collect a little loot, if you don't collect a trip to the mortuary in the meantime.

I thought over all my unpaid bills.

I thought over times in the past when I'd been tempted to disregard the screwy affinity I have for scenting the

14

nearness of green. Almost like a water-dowser, you might say.

Then finally I thought over all the lumps Doug and Lee Roy had handed me, and the remarks they had made about my height. If the tang of loot wouldn't do it, the insults would.

I walked briskly to the backyard, stumbled across a bird bath, took a chance and dipped a handkerchief in it to sponge my face. I straightened my tie and ducked through the privet to the site of the barbecue.

I fixed a smile on my map and walked toward the copper and chrome rotisserie, around which two men and two gals were seated in aluminum chairs and various stages of intoxication. On a picnic table a shaker of gimlets gleamed in the faint smudge of daylight from the western horizon.

"Hi, folks. Don't mean to disturb the party—oops!" I stumbled over a litter of toy rifles and guns, plastic autos and space helmets denoting the kids already packed off to bed. "—wonder if I might ask you a couple of questions."

A small, neatly packed blonde in short shorts and halter waved her cocktail glass at me. "Jinxie sweetie, who is that? Not another of your miserable friends from the Legion post?"

"Can't see," Jinx was a ruddy young type with bathing trunks and the beginnings of a paunch. He tottered to his sneakered feet. "Who goes there? Advance and identify yourself, neighbor."

"Thanks very much, folks, I—*oops!*" I ran smack into a clothesline that caught me across the forehead. Down at the end, two old Army uniforms slid off hangers. The other gent, a lean individual with thin black hair, horn rims and a dour expression, weaved over unsteadily and hung them up again.

" 'S all right." He blinked owlishly. "Old 44th Armored suit. Hardly fit it any more. Jinx'n I got shafted into marching in the Fourth of July parade. By the way—"

He extended a thin hand. "Alden Quinn. Actuary, Old Bald Eagle Insurance Company. You in insurance?"

"Nope. The name's Johnny Havoc. I'm—you might call it investigating work."

"Have a gimlet," said the other dolly, a thin, bustless brunette wearing a playsuit. She reached for the shaker and missed. "Alden, you do it. I'm on my ass."

"Pleasure." He pressed a filled glass into my hand. "Introduce you—"

The thin number was Alden's wife Louise. The redhead was Judy Gordon, wife of Jinx, who now began pumping my hand.

"Lemme give you my card, Hassock. Maybe you'll need something nice in lingerie for your wife or girl friend. Get you a good deal. I cover the East Coast with Empire State Foundations." He gigged me in the ribs. "Pretty funny, huh?"

Judy Gordon giggled. "Tell him the name of your new bra, Jinx."

"Hol-Dit-Furm. We specialize in broad coverage." He laughed so hard he fell down.

Since Jinx didn't seem ready to get up, I took his chair. The shaker went around again. Luckily the only light in the yard was the soft cherry glow of the simmering charcoal bed. They couldn't see the somewhat ravaged condition of my suit. Alden Quinn hitched up his horn rims.

"You said investigating work?"

His wife sat up. "Oooo, are you a policeman?"

"I'm afraid it's—ah—confidential, Mrs. Quinn. All I can say is that I'm working in—ah—behalf of your neighbor Ned Jones."

"Not any more," said Judy Gordon. "Not since that funny Mr. Bogart moved in."

"Did you say *Bogart*?"

"Pretty humorous, I'd say," Jinx said. "Even curls his lip the same way. Judy tried to take 'em a pie when they moved in. No dice."

"I should say not," his wife put in. "They slammed the

door in my face—Mr. Bogart and that hussy living with him."

"Let me get this straight," I said, scribbling gobbledygook on my pad. "Ned Jones used to live in that house—"

"But he moved out about three weeks ago," Louise Quinn told me emphatically. "He and Ginny, his wife and Junior, their little boy. It was very sudden. None of us realized they were planning to leave. Of course we knew things hadn't been going too well for Ned since he lost his job at the factory. When he got hurt in that funny fight at the Glocca Morra over at the shopping plaza—"

"Fight? You're way ahead of me."

Alden began to poke the coals with a stick, clearing his throat like he was about to give a lecture on insurance statistics.

"Ned Jones is a very nice, capable, hard-working guy, a foreman at Peerless Plastics in Sylvan. He dropped in at the Glocca Morra Tap one night for a six-pack. Next thing we knew, Ginny was over here telling Louise that there'd been a fight, and Ned was down at the County Emergency being treated for a broken arm and leg. He didn't know how the fight started. Neither did the bar's owner, Ham Anderson. Ned lost his job, or at least got laid off. Then one morning the moving van pulled up. Day after that, we had Mr. Bogart for a neighbor. Very secretive individual. Painted all the window wells in the basement solid black." Alden coughed, mildly embarrassed. "I had to learn his name from the mailman."

"But he never gets any mail," murmured Jinx, practically horizontal now.

"Certainly sounds peculiar," I said. "I mean, you folks don't think this move of the Jones family was normal—or do you?"

A cigarette pulsed in the starlight as Judy Gordon lit up. She began to pace back and forth, arms folded across her pert breasts. That was all right, I had to keep my mind on the unfolding facts.

"I wouldn't call it normal at all. Especially since Ned took a heck of a lot of pride in his house."

"If you can take pride in being swindled," added Alden acidly.

"Could you explain that last remark?"

"All these houses—"Alden made a sweeping gesture— "This beautiful homebuyer's heaven on earth was put up by one builder, a crook named Stan P. Porter. Uncured concrete in the cellar—cheap hot water heaters—substandard wiring—no topsoil—We were taken, every one of us. Porter should have gone to jail."

"Now Alden," his wife soothed. "You didn't want to stay in the city. You said the green grass would be good for the children."

"I didn't figure I'd spend half my life repairing Porter's botched plastering!" snapped Alden. "Well, anyway, Haddock, Ned Jones got the worst turkey in the whole tract, and he saved it from its natural state of ruin. Worked night and day. Really made the house a showplace, once he learned there was no guarantee after closing and Porter refused to make good on the work. Even the bank tried to force Porter to repair—no go. The only good thing about the whole deal was the local paper getting wind of it. They damned Stan P. and his misbegotten Olympus up one side and down the other. He can't get another building contract to save his soul." Again Alden waved at the night sky.

"He lives a couple of miles from here, broke. So that's why I say we all thought Ned had settled permanently."

"I suppose when he lost his job he ran out of money," I said.

"Ginny told us as much," Jinx murmured, supine on the grass, his paunch rising and falling slowly, an empty gimlet glass balanced on top. "You can figure how surprised we were when the whole Jones family turned up not four blocks from here in another house, but it's a lot smaller than the one he had before. On Seneca Circle."

"You mean Jones didn't pull out of Olympus Acres?"

"Number 12 Seneca Circle," Judy said. "I went over to see them, naturally—but Ginny was almost as unfriendly as that Bogart person—not herself at all. There's something very peculiar going on. If I were you, I'd certainly keep investigating."

"Come to think of it," said Alden, refilling my glass but giving me a faintly suspicious stare. "You never did say exactly what you were investigating, or for whom. You must be plainclothes from Sheriff Peel's office. We're outside the jurisdiction of the Sylvan police here."

"Confidential," I said sharply, standing up so fast I spilled the gimlet in the grass. "Can't say anything. We're not certain how we want to move."

Alden blinked. "Oh."

"Samples in the house," said the horizontal Jinx with a blissful smile. "Give you good deal for wife or sweetheart. Lemme jus' get up—" The gimlet glass fell off his stomach and he managed to raise his shoulders to a vertical position. With a contented sigh, he fell back and began to snore. I murmured hasty thanks and began threading my way through the toys and hanging uniforms to the hedge.

"You've been a lot of help, folks. Thanks."

"Give my regards to Sheriff Peel," called Alden. "I met him at the Jaycee Smoker a couple of weeks ago and he seems like a hell of a nice—"

I didn't bother to inform Quinn that there is no such thing as a nice law enforcement officer, deeming it wiser to make a getaway while gimlet fumes still muddled their brains. In the bushes I paused to make note of the new address of the Jones group, and to study the house inhabited by the inscrutable Bogart. All appeared safely dark.

I hotfooted it for the carport, confident I had stumbled on a situation fraught with financial possibilities—and forgot everything when I saw what was in front of Bogart's house.

Not that I'd never seen a sleek and classy little TR-3 before. It was the package pacing up and down at the curb, illumined faintly in the glow of the parking lights. That got me.

The dolly's lustrous red hair gleamed like new copper.

She was also equipped with neatly turned calves, maddening hips and a pair of mammaries that were record breakers, all of it neatly encased in a tight aqua linen dress. To top it off, she stood a mere 5 feet, and if you think built dollies of that stature go by every day, you haven't been watching hard.

The motor of the TR-3 was grumbling softly. The girl's high heels clicked impatiently back and forth. I came up beside the TR on the street side, trying to smooth the wrinkles out of my rumpled suit.

"Hello, miss. Uh—having car trouble?"

"Does it sound like I'm having car trouble?" she said in a huff.

I leaned on the door and toyed with the head of a very expensive set of matched woods and irons protruding from a leather golf bag. "No, but sometimes these little numbers don't revv up too—"

"I didn't realize they had mashers this far from the city."

Her husky voice was like premium Scotch on a cold January night, but apart from a mild flicker of interest in her blue eyes when she noticed I was only an inch taller, my message didn't even begin to connect. The real object of her interest seemed to be the closed front door of the Bogart establishment.

"You've got me all wrong," I said. "I'm just curious. Girls like you don't normally stand around on quiet suburban streets blowing their corks."

"What's *that* supposed to mean?"

"Now wait a minute. All I offered was help."

"How are you at rescuing drunken boy friends?" she demanded.

"Drunken—I knew there was something wrong."

"He's been inside for ten minutes. I told him he was a fool to come here in his condition. If I ever date that Judd Abel again, I ought to have my head ex—"

With a crash Bogart's front door opened. Light spilled out. I heard heavy cursing, caught a fast glimpse of Lee Roy tussling with a shadowy figure. Then the screen slapped shut. Lee Roy said something unpleasant and the inner door went bang. At the foot of the steps the guy with whom he'd been struggling picked himself up and tottered unsteadily toward the curb. The redhead forgot all about me, but not about her anger. She didn't lift a finger to give her gentleman friend assistance. Down the walk he bumbled. The nearer he came, the more overpowering was the stench of rye. At last he lurched into the reflected glow of the parks. He propped both elbows on the curb-side door, shaking his head from side to side.

"Threw me out," he said thickly. "Bastards."

The girl walked around the car. There was momentary sympathy on her face.

"Judd, are you all right?"

"Threw me out right on my ass."

As he lifted his head to peer around, his face came into view: a sloping jaw, black hair, flashy good looks. He wore expensive slacks and a sport shirt. His skin was tanned to mahogany, indicating that he worked or played a lot outdoors. There was the start of a handsome purple bruise in his left eyesocket. You couldn't light a match within six feet of him, he was so gassed.

"Be all right when I get what they owe me," he muttered. "Gimme a smoke."

Angrily the girl fished her purse from the seat, put the cigarette between his lips and helped him light it. Abel sucked in a long draught, then shook a fist back at the darkened house.

"Rotten, cheating bastards. They owe me plenty, and by God I'm gonna collect. Can't throw me out like that. I'll fix 'em."

*The people in the house owed him plenty?* Oh, mother.

"Judd, take me home," the girl said sharply. "Or get in and let me drive. You can sober up on the way. I should have stayed home with my stepfather instead of letting you talk me into having dinner. I don't understand any of this business you and Stan are involved in, but I know I'm not going to keep going out with a walking whisky bottle. What's happened to you lately?"

Abel hooked a thumb at the black house. "Ask that bunch of crooks what—hey!" His black eyes focused on me with the mean sharpness of the enraged drunk who finds a target for his rage. "Who's the runt, Winnie?"

"Just a gentleman who stopped to see if we were having car trouble." Now that lover had returned, her sympathy, in typical feminine fashion, had switched. "At least he's courteous. Stand up, Judd! Stop weaving like a skid row tramp!"

Abel squinted at me. "Shove off. The lady doesn't need any help."

"The lady wants to go home. I'd suggest you take her. If he won't, I will, Miss—"

"Winnie Porter," she said absently.

Winnie *Porter*? Stan *P*. Porter? I'd hit the mother lode, just as Abel lurched around the car.

"You'll keep your nose out—"

He let go a wild one that whistled over my head. I gave him a quick punch in the belly. He bumbled against the TR-3 fender long enough for me to open the door. I caught him by the collar and folded him under the wheel. I slammed the door, whacking his knee in the process.

"Drive her home, sponge. Then go take a course in how to treat girls."

"Aggressive little bastard," Abel grunted but he didn't climb out. Winnie took her place in the seat beside him. The flash I got from her blue eyes was worth all the trouble.

"Thanks very much for all your help," she said warmly.

Abel revved the TR-3 and sent it bucketing from the curb, weaving a crooked course down the dark suburban street.

Quickly I recapitulated: Lush Winnie's stepfather had the same name as the cheater who put up Olympus Acres. He and Abel were in business together. The uglies who had taken over the Jones place owed him plenty. That's enough for me, I thought, greedily fingering the expensive five-iron I'd snatched from the bag in the sports car a minute before Abel raced away. There was no time to be lost.

I flung the club into my heap, leaped in and kicked the ignition. Ten seconds later I was punishing my pistons and torturing my tappets, trying to keep from losing the speeding red tail lights of the TR-3 up ahead.

# Chapter Three

THE SPEEDING SPORTS CAR whipsawed from one side of the road to the other. It barrelled through the underpass beneath the freeway I'd taken from town. I alternately said prayers for Winnie and hoped Abel's alcohol level would stay high enough to keep his tongue loose until I got a chance to question him.

The TR ripped by another smaller housing development and into open country. Not for long, though. On either side of the road bulldozers bulked in the starlight. Lighted billboards blandished city suckers to forget their claustrophobia in yet-to-be-built Kozy Kottage Acres on the left and Metropolitan View Hills on the right. What the metropolitan view was, I couldn't fathom. All I saw, whizzing at seventy on Abel's trail, was a sprawled shopping plaza where the neon of Woolworth's and several other establishments, including the Glocca Morra Tap, shined their commercial lights into the wilderness.

A few miles up the pike we buzzed past the village limits of a burg called Sylvan. It featured old houses, drooping maples and glass ball streetlights. After a near collision with a hot rod the TR-3 turned left and swung up a driveway half a block from the main drag. The drive was long and curved, so I felt reasonably safe in parking at the curb. I kept the heap idling and listened for the down shift of Abel's gearbox. He stopped with a scream of rubber. A car door slammed. Crickets harped. Heated voices, Abel's louder than hers, exchanged words. It was too far to hear distinctly.

I whiled away minutes studying the house, a decrepit ruin dimly visible through wild vines tangled in the iron spike fence. On the black expanse of lawn foot-high

24

weeds rustled in the night wind. A gingerbread silhouette of cupolas and a wooden turret stood out against the milky night sky. The story about Stan P. Porter's virtual disbarment from the building profession must be true; all around were signs of lousy maintenance and creeping disrepair.

High heels clattered up a board porch. There was a sudden splintery crash, a feminine curse. A light blinked on in the lower storey. The front screen squeaked and banged.

More roaring revvs signalled Abel's explosion from the driveway. He took off back out the main street, using all he had in the gears. My own miserable heap whined in protest just keeping him in sight.

Luckily he drove only a short distance. He navigated crazily around the shopping plaza's main lot, then aced out of sight behind a blue neon arrow that pointed to Glocca Morra Tap, Parking in Rear.

I jammed on my brakes at the end of a line of a dozen crates parked behind the bar. Abel was ducking through the rear entrance from which issued roistering voices and the clatter of a juke. A creepy feeling hit me as I followed. The lot was dark and smelled of exhaust fumes. At its edge trees rustled eerily. My shoes clanked on double steel doors set flush in the surface of the asphalt, doubtless the entrance for the tap kegs. I breathed a little easier stepping into the bar's back hall.

Rainbow light from a Seeburg sprayed the gloom. A noisy neighborhood crowd, mostly men, was ranged along the stools. Abel had taken a spot at the far end. He sat with head in hands and elbows on the mahogany. He shouted for the bartender. He had trouble being heard. Several of the other celebrants had run out of beer at the same time. The only bartender in sight was hopping hysterically around, filling steins and orders.

I'd stopped where the back hall opened into the tap proper. I was lounging with the five-iron in my hand when the door of the Gents banged behind me. I almost hit the floorboards.

I stumbled to catch my balance. "For God's sake watch —Oh-oh!"

'You got a big fanny for a little squirt," said the carrot-haired mastodon scowling down at me. "Right now it's in the way. Haul it away, sonny."

I almost stepped aside, but the bullying thrust of the big galoot's jaw irritated me. So did his minuscule eyes, porcine chin and swag belly beneath his white bar apron.

I hefted the five-iron suggestively. "That any way to talk to a customer?"

He snorted. "You won't be a customer if I throw you out on your ass."

I grinned and swished the iron back and forth through the air.

"Try it, Fatso. I've got an equalizer."

"Hey, for God's sake, Ham," yelled a customer at the bar. "Cut the temper and come fill the damned glasses."

"Yeah, Jeez," cried the harassed bartender just serving Abel a double shot. "These guys got me dancing around so much, I feel like a virgin with hot pants."

Bulge Stomach seemed uncertain about what to do— crack me or relieve the jam in front of the taps. I showed him the iron head again.

"Howsabout it? Want to go a few falls?"

One of his pig-knuckled hands indicated the back door. "Out."

"Ham, for the love of pete, relax," another customer bawled.

"Pick on somebody your own size. The guy wasn't doing nothing."

"Yeah, Ham, you shoved him first."

"Cross sonofabitch these days, ain't he?"

The sudden transformation of the impending fight into a topic for public debate staved it off. Ham glanced nervously at the faces ranged at his bar, most of them snickering over his display of ill will. Savagely he rubbed his palms clean on his bar apron.

"Would you mind letting me get back to the bar—*sir*?"

I stepped aside.

"Not at all. Would you mind serving me?"

"No, but if I catch you starting any trouble with that club I'll break your lousy—"

"Ham, lay off!" began the chorus anew. The harried owner rushed behind the bar and began filling glasses at a frantic clip.

I prepared to move up the bar into the safety zone policed by the other bartender, wondering if Ham Anderson's recent siege of bad temper was still another piece of the murky picture puzzle I'd dumped out of the box tonight. Suddenly a new voice hissed in my ear:

"Quite a performance, Havoc. Must you despoil the suburbs too?"

For a moment I didn't recognize him without his fusty blue serge and battered Dobbs. But one glance at the long nose, the spaniel eyes, the thinning hair and the moist cigar in his eternally glum mouth refreshed my memory. The rest of the outfit—rope sandals, zany gray pants with silver flecks and an electric blue sports shirt—had thrown me off. Clutching a six-pack of Budweiser under one arm, he looked even more helpless and put upon than usual.

"My goodness, Detective First Grade FitzHugh Goodpasture. Or are you his double? They say everyone in the world has—"

"Do I make you nervous, Havoc?"

"Why do you say that, FitzHugh?"

"You always turn on that talking machine you call a voice when I've got you in a corner."

"But I'm not the only one out of his habitat. Commissioner finally caught up with you, eh?"

"Very cute, very cute. For your information my sister Hazel just had a baby. I took a few days off to help her husband look after the kids over in Olympus Acres."

"Oh-oh."

"What's that mean?"

"Skip it. It never fails, that's all."

"Well, you certainly put on one of your typical shows a minute ago."

"Listen! That big ape—" I lowered my voice precip-
itiously; the ape had ears and they were turning red. "Us
little guys have to defend our honor."

FitzHugh cackled. "That's a hot one. You probably
charged your mother a fee when you ate your pablum."
Irascibly he thrust his nose under mine. "Havoc, I'm a
personal friend of Buster Peel, the sheriff, and I think I'll
just call him up as a favor, to tell him what kind of riffraff he has in his county."

"Who said I was staying for more than one drink?"

"You never go anywhere without larceny in your
greedy little heart. And you never leave until some poor
sucker has his bones and bank balance picked clean."

"Unfair! All I did was defend—"

"Never you mind." FitzHugh trundled toward the front
entrance. "That little routine with the iron shows me
you haven't changed one bit. Oh, if you only had a
license! I'd haul you before the state board so fast."

"Dammit, FitzHugh, come back here! I haven't
done—"

"Not yet maybe," he called back. "But the local law is
going to be fully prepared."

I sighed. FitzHugh was a top cop. The only trouble
was my regard for law as somewhat plastic had brought
me up against him a couple of times, and brought him off
looking less than successful. Well, the current problem
was Abel.

His stool was empty.

I rushed to the place he'd been sitting and leaped onto
the leather immediately adjoining.

"Double Scotch on the rocks. Where's the joker who
was here a minute ago?"

"Don't wet your jockeys," said the unhappy bartender.
"Jeez, every time somebody goes to the head, there's a
riot."

"Gimme 'nother," said a voice behind me.

Judd Abel lurched onto his stool. He propped his arms
on the bar. They promptly slid out from under him. His

cheek crashed into the edge of the bar. With that smarting him, he had to go and discover me.

"You! You're the little creep who—"

"My God, drink this!"

The bartender thrust a double portion of rye into Abel's hands, then seized my lapels.

"Better pull out, mister. You seem to be causing a lot of trouble. We had a bad fight in here a few weeks ago. One more insurance claim and—"

I brought the five-iron into view.

"I only wanted—"

"Not that, not that!" cried the bartender.

Abel slapped down his drink. "I'll cream you, you meddling little mother."

"For doing you a favor? For returning this?"

Abel blinked fuzzily. "Wha'd y'say? Tha' mine?" He snatched the club. "Where'd you get it?"

"Fell out of your TR. Look, don't get sore. You lost it when you drove off. I followed you to return it. Hell, I hate to see a guy lose a good club from a set. But if all I'm going to get from you is a cheap display of temper, forget the favor."

I slapped a bill on the bar and pushed my shot aside. "Drink it yourself."

Abel put on a bemused smile. "You a golfer?"

"Nah, I'm a spy for the Kremlin." I sat down again. "You think maybe I go around returning clubs because it says so in the Boy Scout manual?"

Abel sniffed. "I useta shoot in the 80's. When I could afford to shoot. Hey, wa' minute. You were puttin' the arm on my girl—"

"I stopped to see if there was any trouble, that's all. I was doing collection work in the neighborhood. Let me buy you a drink. Then I have to head the hell back to town."

"Well, I dunno—"

Abel fished in his pants pocket, discovering he had only a little change. His smile got fat.

"Well, okay, if you insis'."

He downed the double on the bar without batting an eyelash and poked a finger at my chest. "Then I buy you one for the favor, 'kay?"

I glanced artfully at my watch.

"Well—okay."

I should have guessed his temporary coherence was just that—temporary. But I was edgy about playing on his quicksilver temper too fast. I let the next round come, then the round after that, gabbing with him about the day's ball scores and the latest hullabaloo at the United Nations. Before I knew it he had drained the oxygen from his fast ride out of his system and replaced it all with booze. He launched into a muzzy monologue I couldn't stop. No matter what I said, he just mumbled and went on talking.

"Lotsa goodies in that house, by God."

"Goodies, Judd? What sort of goodies are you talking about?"

"Can't touch. Thick's thieves."

"Speak up, old buddy. You're mumbling."

"Lozzy friends," he said, poking my chest and staring right through me into some distant DT's landscape. "Lozzy, tha' Boger, tha' Porer. I got plenny comin'. You lookin' at man got plenny comin', friend."

"Plenty of hangover in the morning, you mean."

"You know Porer? You know tha' bassid?"

"Uh, no, I'm afraid I don't, Judd buddy. Who's Porer?"

"Man ruin me, thass'oo. Failed. He failed, floppo. Wipe out. Oughta go affer Porer. Can' do it. Like tha' li'l Winnie too mush. Cue li'l twist, real dollbaby."

He reared up on his stool, eyes alcoholically aflame. "But by God I can go affer Boger. I know plenny, buddy boy. Heard 'em talkin'. I'm like a ellfant, never fergit. 'S forshun in tha' house. Part's mine. Take it from tha' suvbish Boger if it's lass—" He seized his temples and began to moan. "Jeez! The jets jus' took off downa runway. Mus' be doon max three leas'—"

"Hey, Judd buddy, stand up there. Let's rustle up some coffee."

"Woops! Pilot, stop bankin' goddam plane!"

"Let's get off the plane, Judd. That's right. Stand up. See? We've landed."

"So we'ave. Whish way eggsit? Make nex' one coffee or I won't be able keep goin' and really give you lowdown on this Boger, th' bassid. Oh, he is one. Cheated me outa forshun, forshun—"

Another five minutes in the Glocca Morra Tap and he'd have passed out cold, so I salved my conscience by telling myself I was doing him a humanitarian service. He clutched the five-iron in his fist as I propelled him bodily past the Gents and into the pitch dark parking lot.

After the twinkle of the back bar, it was hard to adjust the bulbs for a second. I could only see Abel's sketchy shadow bumping rubber-legged against the saloon wall. The crickets harped in the trees beyond the parked cars.

Trying to shake Scotch fumes out of my skull, I said, "Abel, you hear anything?"

"Kill bassid Boger. Foreshun—"

I grabbed him. "Let's get out—"

The sap out of the dark whistled over my head and smashed him in the teeth. I hadn't been wrong thinking I heard a furtive scrape of shoes. I tried to turn, unwind myself. I stumbled.

The second application of the sap caught me solid and solved all my problems in one fast ride down to the black pavement.

Imagine hearing bird calls.

I hadn't heard birds in their native habitat for years. I reflected upon this curious fact as I felt a chisel start to work inside my head.

My cheek was lying in a bed of soggy vegetation. Cautiously I opened an eye. The slant of orange morning sun through a woodsy scene made me still more curious. The air was cool, damp, redolent of early morning.

I stretched, ignoring the skull chisel. I stumbled to hands and knees, sucking long gulps of air. I wagged my head slightly in both directions. It still worked. A bluejay scolded me from a hickory limb. I was about to make some smart crack to the bird when I saw him.

Abel lay face down on a carpet of dewy grass. Someone had bashed out his brains. The tool used, streaked with dried blood and not two feet from his lifeless body, was the five-iron I'd gone to such trouble to return.

# Chapter Four

I SPENT THE NEXT few minutes feeding on a crumpled weed and wondering why in hell I didn't go into some thoroughly dull field like cost accounting. There's something about a dead body—I've seen my share—that punctures the ego like a pin in a balloon. All of a sudden the noisy bluejay on the branch overhead seemed just as important as J. Havoc and his chintzy get-rich-quick schemes; maybe even more so.

From the quiet of the countryside and the momentary absence of nearby motor noises, I figured that discovery was unlikely. Carefully I tore up the butt of the weed, balled the paper, ground the tobacco under my loafer heel and made a circle of the clearing, hunting for evidence of who might have done the work on Abel. I had a stinking good suspicion—whose boys acted the most professional?

I discounted a chance mugging, else I'd have been robbed and maybe batted to death as well. But I couldn't prove Abel had been killed because he was a troublemaker, especially after the lonely woods produced no evidence except a slightly worn trail indicating how the murderers had dragged us in. After Abel's mouth was shut, the hoods probably figured I'd hotfoot back to the city cringing all the way.

Taking a last lonesome look at the corpse—Abel hadn't been such a bad guy; who wouldn't get tanked after being defrauded of a fortune?—I began to trudge back along the footpath. A minute before I'd heard the sound of something like a semi hauling by, perhaps a half-mile away. I promised myself I'd even up for Judd Abel's kill.

33

Maybe I'd been the one to finger him, if his antics at Bogart's house hadn't done it already.

Oh, sure, I was being a hypocrite. I was still on the scent of the green. But I meant what I thought about the dead man, too. A greedy bird like me has to be guided by human kindness at least once a year, or self-respect goes on the wing.

I came from the footpath into a poplar grove on a hill. At the bottom a highway snaked into the distance. Far to the left lay the asphalt parking lot of the shopping plaza. Off on the right, a smudge on the horizon, shone the orange steel undergirders of the freeway arch over the road to Olympus Acres. That the hoods hadn't gone to much trouble to travel the evidence into unknown quarters tipped off their own cockiness, and made me love them even more.

Jamming my porkpie under one arm—stray drivers always notice touches like that, and yawp to the law as soon as they spot an item in the paper—I trudged along the road's shoulder. I was aching mightily by the time I got to the plaza.

Not one car was parked in the whole desolate expanse. I limped around behind the Glocca Morra and found my heap untouched. It was twenty of six in the morning.

Under the front seat I keep a bottle of Pinch for just such emergencies. After a liberal swallow, I kicked the ignition and headed for the village of Sylvan. Over the first rise I met my first milk truck. I'd exited the plaza none too soon.

For a second I was tempted to go straight to the cops until I remembered that FitzHugh Goodpasture had promised to talk to Peel. Besides, Sylvan County was a strange bailiwick. Detention by rubes in the Sheriff's Office might cause my share of the green to vanish abruptly. Whatever Bogart and his ruffians were doing in the Jones house, it was a cinch they weren't planning to be in residence for months and months.

I was taking a chance the green would be negotiable, of course. Guys who won't gamble like that belong in cost accounting. Things weren't good now, but at least I was still a free agent.

A billboard at the village limits of Sylvan announced that the new Olympus Acres Community Park (turn back two miles) would be dedicated on the Fourth by none other than Lt. Governor Thurston Sapinsley, himself, immediately preceding a mammoth fireworks display. I couldn't care less. I had the shakes over the matter of prints on the five-iron.

I breathed a little easier when I remembered Abel had been handling the iron when we came from the Glocca Morra. Unless the hoods had pressed the thing into my hands while I was bye-bye, I was clear. And even if they had, I figured it would take Sheriff Peel's rural experts time to check mine through my Army records in Washington which was, thank God, the only place I'd been printed.

As the sun climbed up behind the pleasant elms and maples lining the main drag of the village, my headache began to increase in direct proportion. By the time I buzzed through the downtown section I was developing symptoms of double vision. Two headed parking meters sprouted four.

I managed to reach the far edge of the village and cram the heap into a slot in front of a twelve-unit curtain wall horror known as the E-Z-Doz Motel. The manager allowed they had a single left. I flung him a bill, and a song and dance about traveling all night for Hol-Dit-Furm Brassieres. I signed a phony name even though not much could be done to falsify the registration of my heap. I was beyond caring.

I tottered into the cubicle, took a feverish bracer from the Pinch, set the precious goods on the night table, pulled the drapes neatly and passed out.

After several false starts I stood up in all my blue and purple glory around four that afternoon. The sight confronting me in the mirror was hardly meant to soothe.

Lee Roy and Doug hadn't left a trace on my puss, but

elsewhere I was Technicolor. I felt it, too. Turning on the hot tap, I boiled nine tenths of the soreness out of my bones. Then I sprawled on the bed and consoled myself with Pinch to wait until the sun went down.

I only made it to seven, because I rapidly became smashed on the hooch and my stomach shrieked for food.

I risked a twilight meal at a café in Sylvan, gnawing the T-bone so ferociously I thought the waitress would charge me extra. Then I ambled down to the corner smoke shop. A copy of the *Sylvan Gazette* on a wire rack told it: MAN MURDERED IN WILLOUGHBY'S WOODS.

The sub-head filled in the unpleasant details: *Golf Club Assassin Still At Large.* Tipping my porkpie to a couple of elderly ladies clucking over the gore, I hauled it back to my head and barrelled out for Number 12 Seneca Circle, Olympus Acres.

The new house inhabited by the Jones family was considerably smaller than their former property. It evidenced all of Stan P. Porter's gimcrack construction and none of the saving touches of Jones himself.

The scene down in the next block was even more picturesque: Saw horses had been placed across the intersection. About a hundred suburbanites milled in the blocked off street, poking at charcoal grilles, staggering around big beer casks on trestles, lounging in various stages of undress at picnic tables brought to the front lawns. There was even a Sylvan County Sheriff's Department car parked at the corner. The officer responsible for directing non-existent traffic was jollying it up with several suburbanites, tin beer pail in hand. Over the whole scene floated an unlikely blend of Sinatra, Mulligan and Wayne King amplified from an assortment of woofers and tweeters. The block party made me nervous; I didn't care for the presence of the law.

I went up the Jones walk.

"Mr. Jones isn't home, pops."

"Oh. I see." I frowned at the teenage snippet who had answered my ring. "When do you expect him?"

"Soon as they run out of sauce down the street."

"Jones is at the block party?"

"Who zat, Ursula?" piped a youngster in the living room.

"Just some salesman, Junior. Be quiet."

"I'm not a salesman. It's important I see Ned Jones right away."

The snippet took a stick of gum from her clam diggers and folded it into her Revlon maw. She rubbed the toe of her left sneaker reflectively against her right calf. Her look made me think I was wearing a celluloid collar.

"For fifty cents an hour, I don't have to run errands, pops."

"You'll run this one. Go get him."

"You can't order me around. How do I know you're not some kind of sex deviate? Hell, I read *Lolita*." She started to slam the door.

I inserted my loafer and got my toes crunched before I added my shoulder and busted into the foyer.

"I've a good mind to flip you over and slap your bottom, the way your old man should have done ten years ago. But I hate crowds. So there's a five spot in it for you. Now you trot down and fetch Jones."

"Try and make me."

With a leer I said, "You don't want to do it for five bucks—let's see if a good paddling will turn the trick—"

I lunged.

"Okay, okay!"

Ursula wiggled past and bolted out the front door on flying sneaks. I scaled my porkpie onto a chair and stepped into the living room, rubbing my hands.

"Well, well. Hello there, little lad. What's your name?"

"Junior."

He was all of eight, a blue-jeaned, T-shirted kid with a mug like a young Jack Dempsey and the warmest pair of brown eyes you ever saw. Those eyes and his freckles almost made me want to go into fatherhood.

He menaced me with the latest creation of the Mattel

weapons trust. "Stand back or this ultrasonic ray'll fry your brains."

"No more than they've been fried already. Could I sit down and wait for your Dad?"

He screwed up his right eyesocket suspiciously.

"Dunno. You bawled out Ursula—"

"Anything wrong with that?"

His face brightened, toothless gaps and all.

"Naw. She's a meanie. All the time trying to make me go to bed and saying she'll call the FBI if I don't brush my teeth."

"Nasty child," I said, settling down on a sofa. "Don't worry about me. I'm your Dad's friend. Soon as he comes back, I'll get out of your way so you can go to sleep."

"I told you I didn't want to go to sleep."

"What would you like to do? Fry my brains?"

With a smirk he flung the toy into the corner and reached under a leather lounge chair, coming up with a stack of comic books.

"I wanna read. Dad doesn't like me to keep 'em around, so I don't get much chance. Want one? Superman, Plastic Man, The Flash? All swell."

"How about the Blue Beetle?"

"I never heard of him."

"Never mind. I'm showing my age. Look, Junior, your Dad's right. You could do a lot better than comics. Why, I can tell right away you're a smart youngster. You should be reading good books. You can learn all sorts of things from a good book." I didn't mention I meant ways to make money without working.

Junior perched on the sofa arm. "Name one."

"Well, how to fry eggs on the bottom of a tin orange juice can in the woods, for instance."

"*I* hate eggs. And you sound just like Dad. Why are you preaching to me?"

"Hell—uh, heck, Junior, I don't know. I guess I just like you. By the way, my name's Johnny."

"I don't like you, Johnny. I don't like that book bunk."

"Then you don't know which way is up, my young

friend. There isn't a book in creation that can't be useful in some way. I may not look like much of a scholar, but I've learned plenty from books." I neglected to tell him the books were biographies of Arnold Rothstein, P.T. Barnum and Yellow Kid Weil.

Junior cocked a disbelieving eyebrow.

"*Any* book?"

"You name it, it's useful. Take my word."

He gigged me in the ribs. "Put up or shut up."

"Did Ursula teach you to say that?"

"Naw, Dad, when he used to have his poker club, before the accident and he got all grumpy and started going into the bedroom and shutting the door to talk to Mom. Don't change the subject. There's a lot of old books in the cellar. I'll pick one. Bet you can't show me how I can get anything out of it but a headache."

I glanced at my watch, wondering how long it would take greedy Ursula to carry out her mission. Junior grinned at me like the Grand Inquisitor. I'm a sucker for kids with freckles.

"Bet, Junior. Go pick a book."

When he clomped up from the basement blowing dust off a mildewed volume with curlique gilt letters on the spine, I knew I'd let myself in for it. The title plate announced, *The Wonders of Mammoth Cave, Kentucky*, by someone named Harve Phiggs. The copyright line was 1921. What did I know about Mammoth Cave then or anytime?

Junior rubbed his hands together, stuck a finger in the damp pages, flipped the book open.

"Go on, Johnny. Read me something to help me out in Little League."

"Now wait a minute!"

"Aw, you're just a big blabbermouth after all."

My pride was injured. I hit a line of text blindly and began to read aloud:

" '. . . Upon motoring to this scenic wonder of the American Midwest, however, the cautious tourist must be alerted to certain dishonest practices designed to lure him from reaching his long-sought destination.' "

Junior covered his mouth and giggled in derision.

"Hang on," I mumbled feebly, "it gets better." It only got worse.

" 'At various sites along the highway leading into the National Park, persons appearing to be park personnel, through the device of official-looking uniforms, wave the motorist to the side of the road, as though welcoming him to Mammoth Cave. These persons have no connection with the park service. But by the time the unhappy tourist discovers this, he has already been blandished into purchasing a ticket for a tour of one of the smaller, less impressive caves in the area. A close inspection of the badges worn by these imposters will prove them to be nothing more than shields issued to honorary police auxiliary, or some such other useless and antique honorific. However, these men, generally of the fast-talking 'slicker' type, are extremely adept at mulcting . . .' "

"You read enough awready."

"We're just coming to the useful part."

"B'loney."

"Listen, Junior—" I grasped at straws. "Suppose you wanted to run a little business. A lemonade stand. Penny a glass. But all the kids walk past your stand. So you put on a police badge like you buy in a dime store and—"

The tadpole's eyes lighted with a larcenous gleam that warmed my heart. "And I tell 'em I'll arrest 'em if they don't stop at the stand, huh? It'd only work on kindergarteners. By the time you get to first grade you're all wised up to Santa Claus and sex and things like that."

"You are?"

"Sure. Hey, Johnny, read some more."

"Well, okay. It says on down the page—"

Junior grabbed my arm. "Somebody's coming up the walk."

I leaped up as the screen banged. A slender, sandy-haired young type with glasses and his right arm and left leg bundled in casts hobbled into the room on a cane, followed by a trim brunette in slacks and sweater. The dame rushed forward.

"Junior, are you all right? Is this the man—?"

"What the hell are you doing in this house, mister?" asked Ned Jones. "Speak up! What's your business?"

"Jones, let me explain—"

"That the man, Ursula?" said a bullfrog voice outside.

"He's the one, all right. He made lewd remarks and offered me money."

"By God, you teen-age monster, get inside here and I'll paddle the—oh-oh!"

"You'll do *what*, mister?"

Bullfrog hoisted his ponderous corporation as he rolled through the door. Over his shoulder he said, "Go home, Ursula. You'll get paid later. We may want you in Sylvan tomorrow to write a complaint. I'm certainly glad I dropped in on the block party when I did."

He looked back at me. "We don't take to sex maniacs in this county, friend. Especially when they have the stamp of city riffraff all over them." He hitched up his Sam Browne and displayed his star. "I'm Buster Peel, Sylvan County Sheriff. And you're in trouble."

"Sheriff, I only stopped to talk with my friend Ned about—"

"He's lying," Jones cut in. "I don't know this man."

"He's *my* friend," Junior cried. "His name's Johnny."

"Oh, Junior!" His mother Virginia held him close. "To think what might have happened if Ursula hadn't found us and we hadn't found Sheriff Peel."

Peel extended one porcine hand. "Take out your wallet and hand it over."

Suddenly he saw my porkpie lying on the foyer chair.

"Hey! That city cop who phoned me last night—Goodpasture—wait a second! Your name's Havoc! Goodpasture said you were acting nutty with a golf club and—Good God! Willoughby's Woods! A *golf club*—!"

Virginia Jones covered her face and let out a shriek. I

knew when it was time to talk and time to act. One shove and Buster Peel sprawled against the closet door. I ran out the door. But it didn't take Peel long to recover. With barely five seconds in my favor, the chase was on.

# Chapter Five

HELPFUL URSULA SCREAMED like an air-raid siren. Sheriff Peel whammed into her as he hipped it down the front sidewalk. They went paunch over sneakers into a petunia bed. Down in the next block at the sawhorse barricade, Officer Simms craned his neck, no doubt wondering why I was running straight toward him.

Responding to Peel's bellow, Simms leaped under the wheel of his car, then leaped out again as another of Peel's apopletic hollers informed him he'd done the wrong thing. Running fast as my sawed off legs could carry me, I decided I'd try to lose the law in the confusion of the block party, gain time, then double back for my heap.

This raised anew the problem of Officer Simms, however. He was a big hunk of muscle, and already unlimbering his side arm.

I threw up my hands. "Don't shoot, don't shoot!"

Braced spraddle-legged in front of the barricade he bawled, "Give up?"

"Not this Sunday, Clarence," I said, and dove between his legs on all fours.

Officer Simms would have pumped a slug into my hipbones had not several suburbanites been jitterbugging only a yard or so behind him. He leaped the sawhorse. I did a fast bolt across the community dance floor.

Simms roared, "Stop that man! Somebody stop him! He's homicidal!"

Just as I was gathering a fair lead through the dazed crowd, a pair of perfumed arms snaked around my neck. A wife of Amazon proportions peered down with big violet eyes.

"Kiss me, handsome. I can't stand this damn P.T.A. pose any longer."

43

"No, lady, I—*ulp*."

In other circumstances I would have enjoyed it, because she had a blouseful of goodies which she lavishly bestowed on my chest. Out of the corner of my eye I saw Simms bulling through the giggling dancers, closely followed by Sheriff Peel. Someone grabbed my shoulder.

"You little masher—!"

I ducked. He punched his wife in the eye. She reached for an available picnic table and came up with a bowl of potato salad. The husband slipped on a beer can as the potato salad sailed through the air. Simms had turned his head searching for me. Buster Peel was directly in the line of fire. Guess who got it in the face.

Peel howled like he'd been emasculated. In a dither, Simms tried to help. I pelted on through the mob. It had begun to coalesce now, pulled together by the commotion. Not a yard beyond the beer kegs on the trestles a human wall blocked the pavement from curb to curb.

Simms and Peel shouted new exhortations about how dangerous I was, the latter with mayonnaise in his hair and murder in his eye. I had worked myself into a corner. If I cut to the lawns on either side, the cops would surely veer and haul me down. Simms was a strong runner, pounding closer every second through the obstacle course of picnic tables. He kicked over a portable hi-fi and kept running while Bobby Darin ran down to a gurgle.

The only way out was through the crowd. They edged closer every second, most of them treating the sight of Simms with a gun as hilarious spectacle, thanks to the booze that had flowed all night long. Then I saw a bung starter on the ground.

Three of the kegs hadn't been tapped. I tapped them, one, two, three, and jumped out of the way as a river of beer inundated Officer Simms.

When Simms fell, his pistol went off. Someone in the crowd screamed. The mob split in half. Fumbling around in the foam, Peel threw Simms' gun away and howled there'd be hell and damages to pay if they shot any bystanders. Simms shrieked in return that I was getting away. I certainly was.

On the other side of the rift in the crowd I zipped left up the nearest lawn. The front door of the house was unlocked. I barged right in. Immediately another broad began to scream.

"It's my husband, my husband!"

She grabbed her bra and tried to cover herself. Her surprised lover stood gaping with his Bermudas awry. When he discovered I wasn't the cuckolded party, he got mad and pitched a heavy vase at my head.

So full of bourbon he smelled like Kentucky, the bruiser clamped hands on my windpipe and shook me from side to side, cussing me out for daring to interfere, being a Peeping Tom, etc. etc. The broad scampered back into her panties and released another piercing shriek.

"Leggo, you stumblebum," I yowled. "Take your hands off—*brrrack!*"

"Come roun' snoopin', will you, fink? Fix ya—"

"Let me—*brrrack*—Stop chok—*brrrack*—You asked for it!"

He got it, too, a Westinghouse fry pan snatched wildly from the kitchen counter, right across his dome. He bleated like a stuck shoat. The front door banged. Simms plunged forward to the attack. I pitched him the fry pan.

He must have thought it was a bomb. He threw up his hands and turned to flee. Buster Peel was just arriving on the scene. Simms collapsed in his arms like a diva faint from all the applause.

The dolly in underwear was hopping around from one foot to another, sobbing her heart out because her infidelity had become a public spectacle. I did us both a favor and slapped down the master wall switch and threw the whole house into darkness.

"Officer Simms, damn you, stop stepping on—"

"Christ, Sheriff—*ow!*—I got my goddamn foot in a planter box and—*oh-oh!*"

The planter box fell over with a loud karrumph. The

language that followed couldn't be printed even by Grove Press.

I skedaddled out the rear door of the house, leaped tomato vines and privets, working my way back down the block to the cross street. There, with no signs of pursuit, I dashed along the sidewalk, pausing only long enough to pry the hood latch on Officer Simms' car and heist the distributor cap.

Halfway back to the Jones residence I came across the sheriff's boat. It, too, I relieved of its vital equipment. I tossed both caps into some mock orange, ran on and bumped into someone in the dark.

"Johnny! Why are those cops chasing you?"

"Junior! Sssh—quiet! It's all a misunderstanding."

"It looks like the burning of Rome I saw on TV once."

"It'll be the burning of me if they catch me. Where's your Dad?"

"Inside. He's keeping Mom safe until they catch you. I snuck out to watch."

"Good boy. Come along to my car. I want to give you a note for your Dad. Don't tell him where you got it. Don't tell anybody else about it, either."

I reached into the glove compartment, got pad and pencil and began to scribble.

"You're my pal, aren't you? My buddy? If you turn me in, I'm cooked. But deliver this to your Pop and I promise it'll help your Mom and Dad cheer up again, maybe even get you all back in the old house."

Junior's teeth shined in a grin in the dark. "Move back on Mohawk Trail? Wow, I'd go for that lots. Anything you say, Johnny."

"Then take this and forget you saw me."

"Right away, Johnny."

He shot up the lawn fast as his Keds would carry him. The front door slammed. I hopped in my heap and chewed rubber U-turning back toward Sylvan. If what I'd written didn't ring the bell, then all the mayhem I'd committed on the persons of Simms and Peel would.

The bell for my funeral, that is.

# Chapter Six

THE HAMMER-HAMMER-HAMMER of knuckles brought me off the mattress like a shot.

I was naked as a jaybird. Frantically I hooked my boxer shorts off the bed post, wondering why in blue hell I'd let myself take a hot shower at 3 a.m. after trying to keep awake all night with the last of the Pinch. Hot yellow sunlight striped the rug of the motel room. It was already mid-morning.

I stumbled for the door. Could a cruising sheriff's car have spotted my heap?

Impossible. I'd parked in a slot assigned to another of the units, a slot behind the building, out of sight of the highway. I hadn't even seen the motel proprietor after I made my dash away from Olympus Acres back through Sylvan, because I'd paid for another night in advance just as a precaution, when leaving the evening before. I doubted the prop would especially remember or think suspiciously of his guest, Mr. Lutz, occupation bra salesman.

But the hammering continued.

The chambermaid? Too early.

Apprehensively I peered out through the venetians.

Cripes. A taxi was pulling away. Outside, Ned Jones, all alone with cane and casts. I'd completely forgotten. With a sigh of relief I opened the door.

"Am I glad to see you, pal."

"I'm looking for a Mr. Lutz who—*you*! What is this?"

"Come in, come in!" I dragged him by his uninjured arm and put my back against the door. He rolled his eyes around, as if checking for hidden assassins.

"Relax, Jones. This is on the level. I need your help

47

and I think I can offer you some in return and I mean the green, spendable kind."

"That's why I came." Jones fished my note from his shirt and threw it on the bed. He pointed. "That's what it says. 'If you want to find out why you were forced from your home, and make a profit at the same time, ask for Mr. Lutz, E-Z-Doz Motel, Sylvan, by ten tomorrow. Come alone and don't tell anyone.' I threatened to spank Junior to make him tell me who gave him the paper, but he wouldn't say. I figured there really was a Mr. Lutz," he finished angrily.

"Who did you think gave Junior the paper, the fairies?"

"Go to hell. I don't have to listen to that kind of lip. I know all about you. Your name's Havoc. You're a city hustler. And I think I got suckered coming here."

"Hold it, hold it. Sorry I wised off. It's just that I've had some rough times lately."

"And given some to the sheriff," he replied. "He wants your scalp."

"How did you find out who I am?"

"Peel told me, after he came back from the block party." Jones couldn't restrain a grin. "With potato salad in his hair."

"Listen," I said, "you didn't spill about the note—?"

"Why should I?"

"Why shouldn't you have?"

"Because, damn it, you said you could tell me why I was stiffed out of my house!"

"So you think you were stiffed, too?"

Jones' eyes got fiery. "It was strong-arm from the word go. Let's not waste time. If you know why it happened, talk."

"You'll get sore again," I said. "But that's all right, because I think we both smell the same skunk. I didn't say I knew why, but I said I could find out. I can, if you'll give me some help."

"I'll help you, right into a cell at county jail. You're nuts."

"Am I? Then why did Mr. Bogart's cronies beat me up

when I tried to locate you at your old place? Why did they follow me when I followed Judd Abel? I only missed getting the dope on what's, in that house because Abel was drunk. Bogart's crowd spilled his brains at the first opportunity and tried to leave me with the rap."

Shaking his head, Jones said, "They didn't try, they succeeded. Have you read the papers? How the sheriff could miss you this close to Sylvan, I'll never know."

It's an old Edgar Allan Poe trick with a letter. The most obvious place—"

"What?"

"Skip it. The question is, will you cover me so I can operate?"

"Operate how? For what?"

"There's something valuable in your old joint. Do you know what word Abel used? Fortune. Not peanuts, Ned —fortune."

"What could it possibly be? The house is a pile of junk Stan P. Porter foisted on me for twenty-three grand. Don't tell me this Bogart, whoever he is—"

"That's another point. Who is he?"

"For a guy who talks like he knows everything, you sure don't know much."

I cocked an angry eye at him. "Maybe I'm the one wasting time. Maybe you just came here because you like cab rides in the fresh morning air."

With a sigh Jones sat down on the edge of the bed. His leg cast with the metal walking stud on the bottom stuck out awkwardly in front of him. His shoulders slumped.

"You got me, Havoc. I'm hurting, bad, right in the time-payment receipt book. I don't know you. You're mixed up in murder but—" He lifted his head. "But I've put my family through hell the last few weeks. If you can help me get back at those thugs who pushed us out, I don't care if you're Beelzebub himself."

I slapped him on the back. "That's the way to talk! Now to show you my heart's in the right place, I'll tell you how I got involved in this mess."

I did, starting with the collection call. He grew popeyed

at the part about the corpse in Willoughby's Woods. Even as I talked, I mentally debated about spilling everything. Yet I had to induce him to trust me, or the scent of green would remain only a scent. If he did walk out and tip Peel, I'd be in no worse trouble than I was in already.

At the windup I said, "There's money in your house, Ned. In what shape and form I don't know. We'll split straight down the middle on anything we recover—reward, old gold, rare books or stereopticon slides. You give me the facts and I'll take the chances on the loot being good."

"Fifty percent?"

"Straight."

"You sure don't mince words about being greedy."

I shrugged. "Call it greed. Call it free enterprise. It's my style."

A reluctant grin edged onto his face again. "I like it. I'd like it better if you could take Bogart and shove him—"

I raised a hand. "Understood. But first, any idea who he really is? Or what?"

"None, I'm afraid."

"When did you meet him?"

"The day he pulled up at the house in his black Imperial. He had that doxy Zelda along. He offered me thirty-five grand for the house five minutes after he walked in. He poked in the bathroom, went to the basement, tried to pretend he was serious about the place. But he wasn't. Only about getting it for thirty-five."

"That's a lot of jack to turn down."

Jones' jaw had a pugnacious thrust. "Money isn't everything. Or at least it isn't when you're working. I put a hell of a lot of effort into the house, making it a decent place for Junior and Virginia from the hodgepodge that crook Porter built."

Briefly Jones sketched what had happened next. Several days after Bogart's initial interview, Jones went to the Glocca Morra for beer. The place was so crowded he could barely move to the bar for a cool one. The next thing he knew he was in a fight. Feet were stomping him on the floor. The whole place exploded.

"I never saw who hit me, even the first time. Just some jokers with chairs and beer bottles. I'll bet anything it was the two creeps Bogart brought with him when he came to see me in the hospital. I'd been there six weeks. I was already strapped. Workman's comp can't begin to cover medical bills and mortgages, payments and groceries and things like that damned Recreation Center. But I guess you wouldn't understand, being single."

"I understand how you have to take care of a nice kid like Junior. Go on."

He did, and it was pretty woeful.

Bogart offered him nineteen thousand, less than the initial sale price, suggesting slyly that Ned had better take it, unless he wanted further accidents. There were no obvious threats. Just subtle as a sledgehammer glances between Bogart and Zelda ("She loves blue roofs," Bogart had said. "She's just gotta have that blue-roofed house") and Doug and Lee Roy.

Jones knew he wouldn't be able to work for a long time. His injuries, while not wildly painful, were breaks of a sort that had to mend slowly; describing them, he rattled off some medical terms way over my head, then told how he finally called a phone number Bogart left and agreed to sell. Only afterward ("It was hell, moving without explaining why") did he inform Virginia of the danger from which he'd tried to protect her.

Virginia wanted to go straight to the police. "On what evidence?" Ned had asked. "Well," she said, "perhaps Ham Anderson could throw some light on who started the tavern brawl—"

"I went to see Anderson," Ned finished glumly. "He clammed up so tight I'm beginning to think he was part of the play. It's bad luck that the extra bartender was sick that night. Only Ham was working."

"Then Ham deserves an interview. Anything else?"

"Nothing else." Jones scowled. "What if you're conning me? What if I never see you again?"

"Look—" I was beginning to dig his solid, purposeful family man style too. "If I don't call in a couple of days, by the Fourth at the latest, you phone Buster Peel and blow the whistle." I fished in my coat for one of the cards with my city apartment address and phone. "This'll tell the law where to start looking for me. How else can I convince you I'm leveling?"

Jones studied the card, then grinned. He held out his hand.

"Okay, you're leveling. I'll take a chance, too."

"Can I count on your help if I need it?"

He started for the door. "You know where I live."

I held the door open but stayed out of sight of the street.

"Thanks, Ned."

"Not yet. Wait till the old place spills the pot of gold." He started limping toward the office to call his cab. He stopped a few feet along the walk. "You know, even if you did con me, I'll have to admit you did a damned good job. But I'm not sure what to tell Virginia—"

"Tell her the note was a fake. What a woman doesn't know—"

"I get it. I'll play it close. Luck, Havoc."

I closed the door without mentioning how much I was going to need it.

When the chambermaid came to clean I hopped in the sack and pretended to be asleep. I stayed under the covers, muttering and groaning like I'd had a hard night. I slipped her one more day's room rent plus two bucks for conveying the goodies to the management. When she left I rolled over on my belly and snagged the phone.

"This is Mr. Lutz. Get me Will Underwood in editorial on the *Daily Times* in the city. And reverse the charges."

When Will Underwood came on the wire he barked, "I don't know any Mister Lutz."

"Oh yes you do."

"Listen, you hustler, why should I pay your phone bills?"

"Because I still have your hundred from that last gin game."

"Oh, yeah, I forgot." Over the wire crackled the racket of the city room. "Well?"

"A party who calls himself Bogart. Rolls his upper lip and—"

"Are you drunk? Or peddling old movies to TV stations?"

"He only calls himself that, Will. Listen, I know he's somebody. I should remember. I've seen his real name and picture, maybe years back, but I've seen it." I fed Will a brief description. "Anything register?"

"Only that you're buggy as ever." Will let out a long sigh. "I suppose you want me to waste my lunch hour in the morgue, all because of a lousy blitz at a cent a point. Well, I don't get any flashes from your description, but what the hell, do you think I memorize every story I wrote a head for? I'll see what I can find. Where can I call you?"

"You can't. I'll call you."

"Oh, it's one of those times, is it?"

"It certainly is."

"City police, country police, state police or FBI?"

"It may be all four before I finish," I said, hanging up.

I went quietly nuts in the motel room during the middle of the afternoon, the time I figured Ham Anderson's bar would be relatively deserted. At three I tooled the heap out through Sylvan without incident. A local law dog scribbling tickets at parking meters didn't even glance up.

The great Atlantic & Pacific was doing a thriving business at the plaza, but the Glocca Morra had none. It was too early for the after-the-factory group and too late for the lady tipplers who take a noon martini with the marketing. Perfect. I drove around in back.

No cars there either. The area was piled high with steel hogsheads fresh from a brewers delivery truck, and

the doors to the underground storeroom were folded
back. A metal chute was in place so the kegs could be
slid to a mattress at the bottom. I peered into the opening, saw only a single light bulb burning among stacks of
empties, and walked into the back hall.

The only inhabitant, a relief bartender I didn't recognize, was listening to the Yanks on the back bar radio.

"Anderson around?"

"Isn't he out in back checking the delivery?"

"Not that I could tell."

"He must be going over the invoice in the cellar. Use
the door just past the Gents."

"Thanks."

I went down narrow wooden stairs into the fragrant
basement, ducking under cool and sweating tap pipes,
walking as noiselessly as possible through the jungle of
cased liquors and beers. Another light burned over a
shabby desk in the rear corner. Anderson had given up
his invoices for a copy of *Playboy*. He had the gatefold
all the way out and was staring at it with rampant lust.
I coughed discreetly.

"Yeah, what do you—hey! What are you doin' here?"

Anderson kicked over the wooden chair in which he
had been sitting. *Playboy* slid off the desk. The breastful
four-color cookie-of-the-month gazed up with litho-
graphed eyes as Ham stepped on her face and started
toward me, his fingers working like steel claws.

"I'm surprised you got the guts to show your face
again, runt."

"You'll be a lot more surprised in a couple of minutes."

That stopped him briefly. "You some kind of plainclothes dick?"

I tried not to show how nervous his towering bulk
made me. "I ought to lie in my teeth, Anderson. But I
won't, because that wouldn't be as much fun as nailing
you on my own. No, I'm not a cop. I'm just a party very
interested in how Ned Jones got smashed up in your
place, and how you didn't see a thing."

Anderson snapped his fingers. "Insurance! A beef over the claim I turned in for the damages after—hell no. I already got the check." A messy little smile of satisfaction, the sort you see on types who pick wings off flies, slithered across his lips. His thick fingers began to work again as he advanced. "You're a nothing. A miserable undersized nothing who came here to needle me."

"Wrong again."

Casually I turned my back and walked toward the square of light formed by the loading chute. While I talked I listened for the slightest change in his breathing to indicate an attack.

"I came back here to tell you that you might have pulled the wool over Peel's head, and over the heads of the insurance people, too, but not everybody is dumb enough to believe you were blind as a little old bat when strangers came into your place and wrecked it and beat up a customer so bad he landed in the hospital. If you didn't worry about stopping the brawl, it sort of figures you had an arrangement with whoever did the brawling. An arrangement that made it worthwhile for you to keep your eyes closed. Now I want to know who—"

Anderson was on the move behind me, cursing.

But a small guy moves faster, on occasion, than a large. I made it to the steel chute in one quick jump. I threw my arms out to either side like a wire walker and leaned against the angle, going up the chute the way I used to climb slides in the slum playground. I spun around at the top and laughed down in his face.

"We can conduct our business a little more politely up here."

"Runt, you don't know what kind of trouble you're biting off."

"And you don't know how fast I can go to the cops if you don't haul your ass up here and start giving me some answers!" I said, bluffing against his knowing I was already in deep with the blues myself. I snapped my fingers. "Come on, lame brain."

Anderson's face fell, gleaming red with sweat. "I can't make it up the slide."

"That's obvious. Use the stairs. I'll still be here."

He ducked out of sight. I settled back on one of the kegs and lit a smoke, smiling to myself in that quaint way I have when I completely underestimate the opponent. I expected Anderson to come waltzing out the rear door the picture of dejection. At the very worst, he might stop at the bar for a bottle or a billy and try to scare me into running.

I heard hammering shoe leather from the other side of a tower of stacked kegs. Anderson bolted through an opening between the kegs and hit my spine with both palms, from behind.

I took a dive on the asphalt. Damn it, why had I forgotten that any bar has two doors? Too late for that, though—Anderson kicked me in the ribs. The force of the kick rolled me over so that I slid down the chute like a sack of potatoes.

I landed on my back on the mattress with the wind knocked out. Anderson loomed against a patch of blue sky. He clamped both hands on the rim of the nearest keg. With a grunt and strain that would have ruptured a weaker man, he rolled the keg toward the chute. I had just about three seconds to keep from being pulped.

The minute the first keg teetered Anderson had another one in place right behind it, then a third, all in one rolling blur.

I kicked out so hard my vertabrae practically came unhinged, arching the way I once did in a high school gym class. The rest of my body flipped up as my soles slapped cement. I went on over, out of balance, bashing my skull on a whisky case just as the first keg hit the mattress full force. The second struck the first, the third hit the second. The impact split all three wide open, even though they were molded steel, and dark beer foamed out across the floor.

Anderson bolted back inside and tore open the door

at the head of the stairs, ignoring the alarmed cries of his relief bartender.

He started down the stairs two at a time. "I'll kill you! You nosy punk. Try to turn me in, will you? I'll smash you—where are you? *Goddamn you, you stinking little son of a bitch, come out and—*"

That's when I let him have it with the case of Vat 69.

Bottles shattered. Anderson howled and slipped in the beer. I gut punched him twice, fast and viciously, snatched an unbroken fifth of Vat from the ruins of the case and whacked him with all my might. The impact cut him down. He sprawled in the suds, moaning, writhing, reaching blindly for me with big, brutal hands. Maybe his King Kong urge would pass in another minute, but I was damned if I'd wait to find out.

I dragged myself up the wooden stairs, shoved the goggling bartender aside and rushed to my heap fast as my tapioca legs would carry me. Only when I was out on the highway, driving like hell, did the shock really hit.

I shook like a bunch of bananas when the monkeys climb the trees. I stuffed a smoke halfway down my throat before I got it lit, and only then realized I'd turned out of the shopping plaza into the lane that would take me back to Olympus Acres.

Well, that was all right. I could use a soothing drive to calm my nerves. Lumps from Doug and Lee Roy I could stand. Foot races with Sheriff Peel I could stand. Almost being minced by a crazed amateur hood was something else again. I wondered idly how long Ham Anderson would last playing in Mr. Bogart's pro league, where the rules said keep it cool.

Suddenly, far up the highway where the underpass cut beneath the freeway, the sun burned and flashed on black metal.

I lost sight of the hurtling black juggernaut as it dipped beneath a rise. I pulled my steering wheel like a wild man, screaming on hot rubber into a dirt side road. I bounced over the shoulder half down into a ditch and

lay there panting as Bogart's black Imperial bulleted
past heading for the shopping plaza.

It was better evidence than a confession that Anderson had helped engineer the beating of Ned Jones. The
short interval between my departure of the Glocca Morra
and the arrival of Doug and Lee Roy whom I'd glimpsed
in the black boat, meant that Bogart was getting very
serious about my presence in the neighborhood. The fact
that the hoods had come wheeling so fast in response to
what must have been one hell of a frantic phone call from
Anderson was evidence that I'd better get out of sight
again fast.

I whipsawed my head back up the grassy shoulder,
nearly tearing out the reverse gears in the process, and
bulled on down the gravel road past farms and cow pas-
tures. The main thoroughfare back to Sylvan was now
unsafe. Consequently it took me a couple of hours to
wind around to the E-Z-Doz.

When it got dark I sneaked down the road to a
packaged goods place to replenish my Pinch. Drinking
Scotch and munching pretzels, I sat in the dismal room
I was coming to hate and tried to plan my next move.

It might have been sensible to pull out and get lost in
the city for several weeks. But the Scotch unlimbered
my muscles and made my encounter with Anderson seem
like a bold bit of derring-do rather than a near miss in
the graveyard sweepstakes. I kept reminding myself that
if Bogart's crew played so fast and hard, it was because
they were playing for a fat pot. Besides, I had promised
Ned Jones.

I swallowed all my doubts in a jigger of final neat
Pinch, put the motel key with its embossed tag into my
pocket and drove through town to the Stan P. Porter
place.

What I expected to find I wasn't quite sure. Perhaps
some tangible hint of the secret of the Jones joint. Maybe
even a piece of evidence I could use to link Porter with
Bogart more substantially than Judd Abel's drunken pre-
death monologue had linked them. The only other alter-

natives were one; going to the bulls. This was nonsense considering the chase I'd led them. Also, Doug, Lee Roy and the rest of the clan could obviously alibi one another. Two; I could storm Fortress Bogart all by myself, but this was impossible principally because I'd always found it safer in my line of work never to pack a heater. If I won, it would be with whatever advantages my skimpy size and overrated wits netted me. Right now, however, prospects for success were lower than nil.

They increased slightly with the discovery that the Porter dump was shrouded in darkness.

I parked the heap in the next block, walked through the iron gate without challenge, and up onto the creaking porch.

I tried the front door. Latched. Marching through weeds that hadn't been mowed in a month, I went around back. The rear porch door was likewise shut tight. A moment later, though, I found a screen with one of its two bottom retaining hooks unfastened. I wormed my undersized index finger through the crack, pried up the other hook and went over the sill with no trouble.

I bumbled around inside the kitchen getting my bearings, sniffing curiously at odors of cobwebs and old wallpaper. The lower floor was mammoth. Enough light filtered from distant street lamps to reveal that here and there—in one of the three sitting rooms, and in the dining room—modern decor had been slapped over the old superstructure. But at some point along the line Stan P.'s past had caught up and the remodeling had stopped.

Unearthing nothing that faintly resembled an office on the first floor, I climbed the broad front stairs. At the far end of a long, eerie hallway, I came across a red-decorated cubicle containing a modern desk and several filing cabinets. I drew the drapes, shut the door and snapped on a glossy brass pull lamp. Then I tore through the desk and files.

The tip-off should have come with the first unlocked drawer. But I'm persistent, and I wasted nearly three-quarters of an hour prowling through miscellaneous let-

ters, shrill duns for payment from various sub-contrac-
tors, gaudy promotional leaflets once used in a direct
mail program for vending Olympus Acres to city dwell-
ers, and correspondence from Porter's attorneys that
chronicled lawsuits pending by irate purchasers.

The files contained more of the same, plus architect's
plans for the single master house Porter had built with
infinite variation and cupidity. The last item tucked in the
bottom of the file and wrapped in rubber bands was a
rolled surveyor's plat of something called the northeast
quadrant of Dado's Pasture, Block 99, County of Sylvan.
On it had been drawn a red circle with grease pencil, up
near the top left corner. Just then auto brakes went
*scree* at the rear of the house.

In a sweat, I slammed the files and headed down the
hallway. Before I could descend the stairs lights flashed
on the first floor.

I cut into a door on the left, a modern bedroom, and
snaked under the bed.

That, of course, happened to be exactly the wrong bedroom.

More lights blazed. I lay with my cheek against the
rug. Suddenly the objects not a foot from my face registered.

A pair of white summer high heels.

In them were tanned feminine ankles.

Faintly stupefied by it all, I watched as one shoe was
kicked off, then the other.

Next came a pair of nylons, with a whispering against
silky thighs that did my hormones no good. Over my
head a deliciously familiar feminine voice was humming a
popular tune. I was thinking of what my first words
should be—maybe I should smile and just tip my porkpie
—when there was a helter-skelter rustle.

A dress and flouncy petticoat plopped on the rug.

I swallowed so loudly I was sure the doll would hear.
Whiz, zip—a bra floated to the carpet. Then a pair of
panties.

With a relaxed sigh she stretched out, crushing my porkpie.

The flick of a cigarette lighter.

A long inhalation.

And me, bug-eyed under the bed.

# Chapter Seven

WHILE I CONTINUED to contemplate all sorts of novel approaches for getting out of the spot, Winnie solved my problem. She flounced over in bed with a contented sigh. Her saucy rump contacted a weak place in the mattress and an unsprung spring jabbed my porkpie painfully.

*"Eeeeeow!"*

I shot from under the rack like a projectile.

"Miss Porter, don't be alarmed—"

She flipped off the pad and rushed into a corner, yowling like a scared cat. I tottered to my feet, porkpie crushed over eyebrows. I yanked it off and caught a delightful scent of perfumed flesh.

Then I caught the not-so-delightful weight of a brass lamp base right across the noggin.

"Miss Porter! For God's sake don't hit me again! I'm not a—"

"Peeping Tom!"

*Whack.*

"Degenerate!"

*Whack.*

"Jack the Ripper!"

*Whack, whack, whack.*

Collectively the blows raised a whanging noise inside my dome. I hopped from leg to leg and saw the little red-haired lovely, unconcerned about being discovered in the altogether, zip the lamp down for one last smasheroo.

"Teach you to come lurking and peeping into—*you!*"

"Watch out for that—"

*Whappo.*

I absorbed punishment across the chops. I landed on

62

my back in the middle of the bed. Right away Winnie dropped the lamp. Shadows leaped crazily on the walls.

She raised her hands to cover herself, but not where you'd have expected. Delicate fingers pressed her lips in complete astonishment.

Despite nuts and bolts rattling around between my ears, I found myself appreciating the ample curve of her hips and the saucy lilt of her positively astonishing mammaries. She was so upset she wiggled and jiggled end to end.

Abruptly she balled her fists and told me to wipe off the smirk.

"I hope you have an explanation for this, Mister—"

Working my bones in unison, I stood up.

"Havoc. Johnny Havoc."

She pointed a finger.

"You were the one Judd almost fought with!"

Her blue eyes flashed unhappily.

"Willoughby's Woods! The golf club!"

She retreated to a dressing table where a petite extension telephone rested.

"Don't touch me, you murdering maniac. I'm going to report you to the police. I suppose you came here to kill me too."

"I did no such damn thing! Miss Porter, listen—"

In no mood to be wheedled, she sprinted for the communicator. In another instant she'd blow the game. I ran across the carpet, clamped my hand on top of hers to prevent her from lifting the receiver. This, however, convinced her I was really lethal.

We wrestled around ferociously. Winnie banged my shins with fierce kicks. Most of her deliciously bare anatomy whacked me at one point or another. I'd have enjoyed it except for the fact that she was scared to death.

I managed to fasten an ungentlemanly paw across her yawp to silence the howls for help. She digested a portion of my hand.

"Now wait, Miss Porter! Stop chewing on me that

way! I didn't kill Abel. The Bozos who did it knocked me out and—"

"Dillinger!" she cried around my hand. "Frank Nitti!"

"Miss Porter, watch those incisors, you're—*yow!*"

She ate practically all the way down to my knuckle. I batted her one. She sailed clear across the boudoir and onto the bed, nude thighs flying. Frantically she crouched among the covers, dragged off the sheet to hide the goodies. I massaged my hand.

"Sorry I slugged you."

"Oh I'll bet you are! I'll bet you wish you'd strangled me."

I dangled the chomped item before her eyes. "I'm just not used to having my flesh mistaken for a short-order snack. Dammit, that smarts."

The beginnings of tears twinkled in her blue orbs.

"Very funny. I suppose you'll wisecrack about poor Judd's murder, too. Did it smart when you struck him over the head, you vicious beast? Why don't you go ahead and kill me? What's one more corpse to a depraved beast?"

That did more than smart. Not that I mind being classified that way. In fact the thrusting breasts she displayed through the sheet encouraged all sorts of depraved notions. But not of the homicidal variety.

I started to explain. She cringed. Disgusted, I went back to the dressing table, dragged out the chair and plunked myself down. After lighting a weed I again displayed my hands.

"Nothing hidden up my sleeve. No daggers, grenades, poison signet rings or siege engines. Come on, hon. Control yourself and let me explain. Don't you want to find out who creamed Abel?"

Winnie sniffed, transferring herself from a defensive crouch to a sitting posture, but still with the sheet draping her curves.

"I don't need to find out. I *know.*"

"Me? Don't be loony. If I'd done him in, would I still be hanging around?"

"How should I know what hideous schemes you're involved in?"

I hitched the chair forward and attempted to demonstrate my sincerity:

"Miss Porter—Winnie. Let me call you that, okay? Makes things less formal. Like I said. My name is Havoc. Johnny Havoc. I'm from the city. Investigating work."

Her eyes rounded suspiciously. "Are you a policeman?"

Not having the heart to lie outright, I replied with a knowing smile. "I don't often appear in uniform." I hadn't, either, since Uncle Sam redeemed the khaki suits he loaned me for two years.

"And you're hunting whoever murdered poor Judd?"

"In a manner of speaking. I already have a good idea of who did the deed. Evidence is another matter. That's why I broke in here tonight. About being under your bed —I didn't know who the hell was coming home so I ducked into the nearest hiding place. It's that simple."

She was repressing some of her frantic behavior. I abandoned the chair, retrieved my porkpie and poked a finger into the dent left by the spring.

"Look what your mattress did to my lid. Cinch I won't make the ten best dressed again this year."

In spite of herself Winnie smiled. "All I can say is, you're the silliest detective I've ever seen." She surveyed me up and down. "How tall are you?"

"Tall enough to cut the mustard when I find a doll my size who—"

A pillow whizzed past my conk and bounded off the plaster.

"Keep your distance! I'm not completely satisfied that your story isn't pure malarky." A frown darkened her pretty brow. "A minute ago you said you knew who killed Judd."

"Right. A couple of city meanies call Doug and Lee Roy. Their employer is one—don't laugh—Bogart. It's all mixed up with a house Bogart stiffed from under a party name of Ned Jones." To pry loose a reaction I added, "Out in the tract your dad put up."

Instead of leaping all over me with hysterical defenses of papa, the redhead peered into some unfathomable distance and talked to herself: "Doug? Lee Roy? Bogart? Those are the men Stan is playing—" All at once she danced off the bed, displaying a tantalizing length of bare thigh, wrapping the sheet around and around for more permanent protection. "All right, suppose I accept what you say."

"Are you in a mood to accent it? Or will you still holler copper?"

She bit her lip. "No. You needn't hover over the telephone. I'll listen, provided you deliver some sort of sane explanation.

I sighed. "Hon, if this caper were sane, I wouldn't be making like Raffles and burgling houses."

"Do you realize you've implied Stan is mixed up in Judd's death?"

"Hell yes. Why do you suppose I came here at all? I know you won't like the nasty thoughts I'm harboring about your old man—"

"May I ask why not?" she demanded haughtily. "I'm as strong as the next."

"But he's your father!"

"Stepfather," she corrected in a way that would have made ice from tap water. "Oh, don't misunderstand. He's treated me well enough since Mom died. But we haven't been seeing eye to eye for quite a while. Ever since he flimflammed those poor people into buying his wretched crackerboxes, in fact. He knows how I felt about his dishonest construction schemes. I came close to moving out. The break—" Her eyes were unhappy. "—is inevitable. But *murder*? That's another story. A very serious one."

I cried, "Did I say Stan P. busted Judd over the head?"

She frowned. "That's a rude way to speak of the dead."

"Ah, hell." I kicked the chair. "I didn't mean it. I'm trying to do a job and get on the right side of you at the same time."

She gave a brittle laugh. "Fat chance."

"Don't blame me for the effort. How many bro—girls do you suppose a guy my size meets? I mean with the right proportions? A cutie with your build is like the mother lode. Naturally I'm interested in your—ah—feelings for Abel, even though he isn't around to defend himself."

She met my gaze with a curious, almost merry twinkle. My hormones suffered extreme agony.

"Well, Mr. Havoc, I understand your problem well enough, but this is hardly the place for romance."

I leered at the bed. "Know a better one?"

"Keep your mind on the track. The clean one. To answer your question, yes, I was fond of Judd. Stop looking like a sheep dog. Not that fond. He was growing awfully boorish. Drinking heavily. As you probably know he was Stan's foreman on the Olympus Acres job. Which didn't exactly endear him to me either. Still, the poor man's dead and whoever did it should be punished. Could we suspend all the flip talk and get down to business?"

Somewhat disgruntled, I said, "You're a hard number, Winnie."

"When it's necessary," she agreed. "Right now it seems necessary. When you helped me calm Judd the other evening, I was rather pleased and flattered. But to find you skulking in my bedroom when you're wanted by the police—"

"You know about that?"

"Who doesn't? The local paper has it in the headline."

I hammered my fist into my palm. "Kiddo, that's why I want to wrap this up fast. For some reason Bogart and his seedy friends forced Jones from a house Stan P. built. They're after something in that house. Money, Green Stamps, uranium, who knows? They haven't found it or they'd have cleared out by now. As long as they don't do the bye-bye bit for Miami or some other sunny clime, I have a chance to nail them."

I failed to mention that my stake in the great crusade

was a share of the loot, whatever it was. Winnie, however, was no dumb cluck.

"Precisely what is your part in all this, Joh—Havoc? Are you a policeman from the city? A private detective?"

"Not exactly."

"Exactly what's that supposed to mean? Oh! A reward? Is that it?"

"Unfortunately—uh—yes. Ned Jones and I have an arrangement. Fifty-fifty of anything we recover. Skip it. Money won't help if I'm socked behind bars for creaming Abel, and that's just what Sheriff Peel plans. Besides, I feel partly responsible for Judd. I was with him when we were jumped. They let him have it and only knocked me out. Dammit, Winnie, you should understand. Little people like us are always pushed around, shoved here, shoved there. The six-footers figure our brains can't amount to anything because we look like midgets. Well, I may be a midget but I can still make a mark."

Winnie's blue eyes teased, not exactly unfriendly anymore.

"My but you're aggressive! And don't beetle at me. I understand perfectly."

I faced her across the bed. "Then will you help me? At least as far as not calling Fatso Peel the second I leave?"

"I'll think about it. State your case."

I picked up my porkpie, set about straightening out the wrinkles.

"It's already stated. I think Bogart—that isn't his real name but it's the only one I know at the moment—is mixed up with Stan P. in whatever is going on at the Jones pad. What's going on is what I came here to discover. So far I haven't. Do you know?"

Winnie's copper curls bobbed, negatively.

"Judd put me on the scent. He mentioned your stepfather and Bogart in the same breath."

Winnie hesitated, placed in the uncomfortable position of selling out her legal relation. I felt like a wretch for forcing her. On the other hand, my pelt was at stake and Abel had already lost his life as a result of the shennanigans. Winnie chewed her lip. At last her head came up.

"Yes, they are mixed up together, Johnny. Exactly how I don't know. Bogart has been here. Tomorrow morning—I started to tell you earlier—Stan is playing golf with him."

A few dozen signals cling-clanged in my head. "Golf?"

She nodded. "Eighteen holes. Stan mentioned it at lunch today. He's going out at six with Bogart and those two primitive specimens he employs." She shuddered. "The one and only time Bogart came to the house, he and Stan spent an hour in the office down the hall. I was forced to be hostess, entertain those two—persons —downstairs. I served them drinks and played records. All they wanted to hear was Elvis Presley. I don't have any of his. Thank God. They drank whisky straight and practically undressed me the whole time."

"Wonder what ever made them do that?" I remarked. She laughed.

"I hate to admit it, Johnny, but I like you. You're brash and vulgar and you don't sound the least bit honest. But when you smile—oh never mind." She gripped my suit, charging up my battery. "Johnny, I wouldn't want anything to happen to Stan that he didn't deserve. After all, people can get mixed up with bad companions."

I thought of Abel. "Sweets to the sweet and electric chairs to those who need electrification. I have to finish this, Winnie, let the grand jury bills fall where they may."

"Oh, I realize that," she said, approaching close enough for the faint vibrations of her mammaries to set up a sympathetic response. "The men who did that to Judd should be punished. I'll do what I can to help you."

"Doll, you've already done plenty. I've been hunting a way to get inside Bogart's fortress without being smeared. That golf match at six is just the ticket. Now you be a good girl and keep quiet about this little interview."

I slipped a hand to her elbow, grew bolder when she

didn't resist. Her eyes were level with mine, a refreshing circumstance.

"Maybe when this is wrapped up we can kick it around. I'm very large for five-foot girls."

She laughed and shook her head.

"Do you bamboozle every one so thoroughly, Johnny?"

"Bamboozle? I resent that. I'm legitimate through and through, every inch a—"

"An operator," she finished lightly. "Against my better judgment, I still like you. If you'd stormed in here six feet tall I'd have called the police. But such a funny little man—"

I grabbed her and gave her a buss.

I expected scratches and toes against the shins. Instead I experienced a delicious taste of cool lips. They suddenly increased their temperature. She breathed faster. Gradually her right hand lifted to my neck. The sheet slipped, slid down the upper slope of her big breasts showing.

"Johnny!" she sprang away. "Did you hear that?"

"Just my glands. Very loud. C'mere—"

She ran across the room, riffled a venetian blind.

"There's a car in the drive. I think—yes, it's Stan coming home."

Her eyes rounded in fright. I heard the crunch of tires, the scree of a brake, the solid chunk of a Detroit-made door. Feet slammed in the downstairs hall. A voice called Winnie's name.

She racked up the blind, threw open the window and pointed, trembling. Stan P.'s heavy tread mounted the stairs.

I stared out the black square. "What am I supposed to do? Fly?"

"There's a rain pipe. Quick, Johnny. If he finds you here—"

Reluctantly I hauled my hocks over the sill, having time for no more than a rapid peck of her cheek which she was too alarmed to appreciate. She practically shoved me out the window.

I snatched at the rain pipe and did a jolly dance against the siding. The window slid shut. The venetians dropped into place. I was left dangling like a participle with the galvanized pipe racing through my fingers.

I braked my lightning descent by jamming my soles against the wall. A couple of seconds later I reached the ground, massaging lacerated palms. I took a last look at the dark window above, wondered whether Winnie Porter would sell me out. The remembered tang of her lips convinced me otherwise.

Six in the morning, eh? A golf game for the fearsome foursome, eh? Encouraged, I hotfooted across the lawn in a mutter of thunder from an impending rainstorm. I hauled into my heap and spent the night in the depressing confines of the E-Z-Doz Motel dreaming of Winnie Porter's anatomy.

# Chapter Eight

*Here Comes Another Load of Guernsey-Good Milk!*
shrieked the message on the side of the truck. The letters
twined around views of repulsive moppets, swallowing
glasses of the awful stuff, and several painted cows. The
artist had painted the cow eyeballs so that they followed
whoever happened to be nuts enough to look at them.
I gave the cows the fisheye right back, slid into the
bucket seat of the empty truck. I was nervous enough
without the assistance of a bunch of four-legged health
bars.

I noted the ungodly hour. A few minutes after six.
Mohawk Trail slept under a lead sky still full of the
threat of rain. I yawned, glanced up the drive where the
truck was parked, heard the rattle of bottles at the rear.
Through the windshield I saw that number 72 was minus
the black Imperial.

Inside one of the Porter palaces some early commuter
turned on the radio. I was treated to Red Foley yodelling
on the farm hour. The last time I had been up this early,
the nurses woke me for formula.

Down the driveway marched the minion of moo, a
husky, dew-lapped old gent in cap and bib overalls, jingling his empties in his wire tote rack. He spotted me,
birdy eyes narrowing.

"What you doin' in my truck, mister?"

"What does it look like I'm doing, firing a Polaris
missile?"

He inspected my heap parked behind the truck. I
forced a smile.

"Friend, howsabout making yourself scarce for an
hour? Take a walk and count your blessings."

I pressed two blessings bearing the numeral ten into his palsied palm. He regarded the bills like black widows.

"Move aside, mister. Here's your dough back. I gotta finish my rounds."

"All I'm asking is the loan of truck, cap and overalls."

I flashed my wallet, riffling through my collection of credit cards. His eyeballs rotated dizzily. "Official investigation. Hush hush."

"You didn't say? What's the trouble, officer?"

"Suspicious party at Number 72."

"I noticed, I noticed! Used to be Jones. Four quarts Guernsey-Good, two quarts Mello-Slim, one pint Nature's Own Half and Half. Jones must have moved. New tenants don't even open the door. Take nothing but coffee cream. Sure, mister, if it's official I'll be glad—"

Naturally that was the moment I missed my lapel and stuffed the wallet into empty space. It landed on the truck floor, wide open. Dewlaps Dewey reached down courteously to retrieve it, and suddenly glimmed a card.

"That don't say police, that says Diner's Club. You sure—?"

"I'll show you my real ticket."

I did. My knuckles. He collapsed. I eased him into the truck's rear, peeled off his uniform. "Sorry, Elmo, but it's absolutely necessary."

Making sure I'd tucked the two tenners under a top button of his union suit, I climbed into the overalls and donned his cap. I had to roll up the pants eight inches. The cap kept sliding over my ears.

Gearing up the truck, I drove it in reverse till it was alongside my heap. Watching all the houses for signs of scrutiny, I hauled Dewlaps across a narrow space into my back seat, then whizzed toward Number 72. So far nobody had peeped outside. That I could tell.

I jingled my bottles, marching up the walk of the Bogart property. Near the rear door stood a galvanized box for the white juice; I discreetly set this out of sight around the corner. Then I pumped the doorbell, whistling and jangling the wire rack some more.

Nothing happened for three minutes. I kept on whistling, jingling and ringing. Finally the door opened a crack. A sleepy female voice muttered unprintably.

"Good morning, good morning, your Guernsey-Good man's here with the milk."

"Put it the hell in the box like always," cried the drowsy Zelda.

"Box? What box? Some kids must have swiped it. We're not allowed to leave milk on the doorstep except in the insulated box. I'll just come in and stow it in your refrigerator."

So saying, I levered the screen door and insinuated my frame through the narrow opening.

The broad retreated across the linoleum. She threw a lock of black hair off her forehead and treated me to a slitted gaze. The kitchen panes rattled as thunder pealed in the sky. I bumbled around in the shadowy kitchen, head down so Zelda couldn't got much of an impression of my face. A doorknob presented itself. The door wasn't fully shut. It opened off the kitchen's center.

"Damn outrage, that's what it is." Zelda fired up a smoke. "Go on, go on, stuff it in the icebox so I can go back to sleep. Why did I let him talk me into moving out here? Golf games, milk when it's just time to go to bed. No, no, stupid! That's the stove. I think. The icebox is the other way. The one with the crown on the door."

I kept my eyes away from the half-awake Amazon, clumped over and opened the box. I thrust some bottles in among a raft of teevee dinners and six-packs. All at once Zelda blinked.

"What are you doing? We don't drink any God-damned chocolate milk."

"Oops, my mistake. I'm new on the route."

Frantically I tried to shut the door so the inside bulb wouldn't light up my map. Zelda thrust an ample hip between it and the box, fussily helped me unload two pints of coffee cream. She wore a red dressing gown that

reacted favorably with her pale skin. It also possessed a
tie-cord hovering on the brink of looseness.

As she wedged the pints among the frozen dinners and
the brew, tumbling, the front of the robe fell away, un-
nerving me with a gargantuan display of creamy flesh.
Two creamy fleshes to be exact.

"There, for Godsakes!" Zelda straightened up, closing
the door. "Now get the hell out of here."

"I'm really sorry I disturbed you!"

"Not that way! That's the cellar."

"Sorry, sorry," I muttered, hauling the door open.

*"I said stay out of there!"*

Zelda reached across my shoulder, batted the door
shut. I leaped back in time to prevent my nose being
clipped off. But I'd gotten a glimpse of some items that
made hardly any sense: hunks of concrete and a heavy
cylindrical drill with handles and a wicked long bit.

"Bogie doesn't allow anybody downstairs, see?" Being
witless, she wasn't really very sore. "Nothing personal,
understand. Mr. Bogart has his—uh—workshop down
there. Lotsa valuable tools. Like—uh—hammers."

"Bogart, Bogart," I repeated, dodging under her arm
where it still reached over my head. "Sure is an interest-
ing name. Just like the actor. Hah-hah. Must make a
note of that name. I'm new on the route."

"Well, give my regards to the boys in the barn when
you—hey! Turn around a second. Aren't you the same
little runt who was here before? The one wanting Jones?"

"Some mistake, lady. The name's Fletcher. Guernsey-
Good." I dived for the exit.

"Guernsey-Good, hell!"

She grasped my collar and hauled me back. Then she
peered down from her pale face, a nutty smile curling
the corners of her generous lips. The more I struggled,
contemplating the necessity of giving her a smack in the
gub if she didn't unloose me, the more unknotted became
the knot of her robe cord.

At last it surrendered completely.

Zelda was faced with the choice of letting go or continuing to display a neck to ankle expanse of flesh. With a giggle she did the former, dumping me on my butt.

My wire rack skittered across the floor. I banged my head on the chromed edge of the sink retrieving it. Meanwhile Zelda had skipped to the back door and was blocking it, half-smiling, all awake.

"Lady, would you excuse me? I have to finish my rounds. It's starting to rain."

The storm broke with another rattle of thunder. Drops tapped the kitchen glass.

"Not until I see if I made a mistake. C'mere, don't keep backing away like a nervous rabbit."

"Lady, unless you allow me to leave this house, I might be forced to act like something less than a gentleman. There are little tots in this neighborhood eagerly awaiting—"

"Don't make me laugh, kiddo. You're so tiny I could take you apart with two fingers."

That was the hell of it. I believed she could. She continued to regard me with a puzzled, dippy expression.

"Wait a minute, it's coming back. I'm sure of it! You're the one those two goons manhandled. Haddock! The collector!"

"Mistake," I growled, lowering my head, determined to batter my way out before it got worse. "Stand aside."

Even playing games, Zelda was a toughie. She clamped a hand under my jaw and pried my head up. Her voluptuous face swam close.

"What's wrong with you, Haddock?"

"I—uh—see Jones isn't here after all. I might as well go."

"Did you dress up like a milkman just to collect a bill?"

"How else could I get into this concrete bunker?"

The more she bent forward to study me, the more of herself she put on display. It was positively maddening. Any other damn time I'd have lined up for a seat in the grandstand.

"I 'member I thought you were cute when you came here before, Haddock."

"Bad light. I'm ugly as sin when the sun's out. Now let me go!"

She tittered. "What's your hurry? Listen, sugar. The least you can do is make up for disturbing my beauty sleep. Gee," she asked, dumbly contrite, "I'm sure sorry Doug and Lee Roy roughed you. The big jerks do exactly what Bogart tells them."

I was free of her grip for the moment but still a hell of a long way from the door. "Is that his real name? Bogart sounds pretty phony."

"Don't you wish you knew! I dassn't tell, either. But that doesn't mean I can't have some fun when everybody walks out on me to go play silly old golf. Don't you think I'm nice? Even just a little bit?"

"Terrific!" I exclaimed, understanding all too well what she had in mind. "Terrific! But unless I latch onto Jones —is that the way to the front door?"

I ducked fast for an arch. The big chick maneuvered in front of me with one lithe stride. That's the price you pay for being born a shrimp.

She flung out her arms to bar my exit. Her robe fell open again. I felt like one of those experimental mice they put through mazes as I barged for the exposed back door.

Once more Zelda cut me off, sliding against the panel a second ahead of me. I smacked into a trace of quivering bazooms.

"Fellas don't usually act this way with Zelda, honey. Fellas usually like Zelda lots. Here we are, all alone, and I just got up and I really don't feel very tired—"

With a cannibal laugh she wrapped her arms around my neck and planted her lips on mine. Her powerful arms lugged me across the kitchen while those educated lips went wild.

Zip, the tie cord failed again.

"Let's go to the couch!" She tickled my ear. "Want a

little eye-opener first? Maybe that'll thaw your cold blood."

"My blood's not cold, dammit!" I howled, feeling idiotic and totally helpless. Oversized gunsels I could handle when I got desperate enough. And law minions and even outraged babysitters. But this mammoth gob of pulchritude with a libido where brains should have been was too much. She crushed the life out of me, hustled me into the living room. We crashed on the couch.

There are limits to chivalry. I doubled my fist and let fly for her chops. She grabbed my wrist before the punch landed, giggling we wrestled around and I lost the fall.

Zelda was on top, mashing me with her gorgeous cans, kissing me every which way.

"Don't be so unfriendly. Gosh, I liked you a lot the first time. Sort of novel. My guys are usually lots bigger. How tall are you?"

"Five feet one and—*ulf*. Zelda, leggo! Dammit, you're—*awwrk*."

Her overwhelming chest banged against my cheek with positively lewd abandon. Her hands went everywhere as she pinched and poked, jabbed and jollied. She seized my ears for another ferocious kiss, apparently guided by the theory that love isn't love unless you snap a few bones.

But before she mangled me, she braced her hands on the sofa and peered down.

"If you aren't the damndest one! How many men do you suppose'd give their right arm to be where you are this minute, Haddock?"

"I *am* giving my right arm. And my right leg. And my left leg and my spine."

She tickled my nose, pouting. "Don't you really want to?"

I grinned feebly. If I couldn't escape her monster clutches by being antagonistic, maybe I could do it by appearing to cooperate.

"It's not that, Zelda. You're plenty attractive. I mean

it deeply and sincerely. But when you plop down that way, and practically cave in my ribs—"

"Sorry." She wasn't in the least. "It's such a novelty, like I said. You being a little shr—guy, I guess I got awful excited."

She smoothed her hair. The smile she threw was lazy, sensual. The time for games was over.

"Now you come here, little man. I'll try not to break all your bones. At least not at first."

The open robe revealed the large white breasts. She wriggled her shoulders. Those mammaries performed all sorts of tricks. She crooked a finger. My innards were marmalade. That's when the bad news arrived.

First slithery tires hissed.

A brake yowled, applied roughly.

Doors slammed. Cleated shoes hit concrete. Zelda's dumb-dolly eyes opened wide. She was no longer amorous, just scared. She wasn't the only one.

Who could play golf in a driving rain? Not Bogart. I found out.

He stamped through the front door followed by the pair of uglies who trounced me once before.

From the expressions on their faces, they were going to be just delighted to do so again.

# Chapter Nine

THE SCENE REMAINED frozen a split second.

But I didn't. Just as Bogart commended some remark about how surprised he was, I lit out across the room, angling for the kitchen.

Doug yelled, "Cool it!"

Not knowing what he carried to back up the command, I cooled it, spun around. The trio of thugs fanned out over the carpet. Lee Roy, piggy brown eyes merry with mayhem, kicked the front door shut on a gray sky already clearing of rain. The patter on the roof had diminished. Another ten minutes and the bunch might have returned to the links. Of such coincidences are funerals made.

I wondered what had become of Stan P. Porter. Had they dropped him at home? Likely. Fat lot of good it did me. Bogart's round, scarred face was nasty. Doug's heater, snatched from the pocket of his damp jacket, quivered in his fist as he worked a cigarillo furiously from side to side.

"A milkman!" Bogart jammed a panatella into his maw. Lee Roy leaped to light it. Bogart puffed, ran his eyes up and down what there was of me. "Isn't that a laugh? I saw the truck out front. I didn't figure Zelda was dumb enough to tangle with a milkman. Guess it's lucky the rain came along to spoil the game after all."

Doug glowered. "How about it, boss? Time for fun and games?"

Bogart shrugged out of his expensive checked jacket, practicing his lip trick. "Plenty of time, plenty of time. Let's have our little conference in private, huh?"

I thrust out my chin to appear cockier than I felt.

"Bogart, I came here looking for a party named Ned Jones. So far all I've gotten from you people is a hard time. I'm sick of it. Tell me where Jones is and I'll be on my way."

Lee Roy tittered. "He's sick of it. Oh, mother, that's rich."

"Yeah," drawled Doug. "He'll be on his way. The midget is a million boffs."

The snide remarks brought me to the point of pitching in with both fists, even against the heater. Some last shred of sense warned me I'd be pretty unhappy in a coffin, even if it was filled with bucks. Hadn't I used my wits before? I could damn well try one last time.

Zelda made it tough, though.

"He assaulted me, honey!" she rushed to lover's side and massaged him with her goodies. "I opened the door so he could put the milk in the icebox. He tried to tear my clothes off."

"What clothes?" inquired Bogart acidly.

I marched to an easy chair, sat down, crossed my legs and smirked knowingly.

Bogart snapped his fingers. "Stand up, little man."

"We can talk sitting down."

Doug allowed me to examine the roscoe muzzle which he placed directly in front of my eyeballs.

"If the chief says stand, you come to attention fast. I got half a dozen lead persuaders here—"

"*Lay off!*"

Bogart shoved his gunsel aside, faced me with wiener thumbs hooked in his belt. Rain glistened in his thinning black hair. His eyes were about as lovely as cesspools.

"Won't listen to my boys, huh? Figure maybe they're just my muscle? Well, that's okay. But when I give an order—"

His paws shot out, helped themselves to a wad of my overalls. He brought me up within inches of his bad breath.

"I told you once to stay away from this house. You didn't pay any mind. You had to come muzzling back. All right. You chomped down on a slice of bread, now you eat the whole goddamn loaf. Zelda! Haul yourself into the bedroom."

"But sweetie, I tell you this little rapist tried to tear all my—"

"Sure, sure. And the moon's green cheese. Haul it!"

He patted her cheek, smiling as tenderly as a tarantula.

"Do like I say, maybe I'll buy you a nice present for holding this creep on the leash."

Zelda batted her ersatz lashes. "You ain't—aren't sore, lover?"

"I should be madder'n' hell. But I know how it goes with those educated hips of yours. And you did me a favor. I won't forget, so long as you mind nice. If he screams, pretend it's night and we're all watching Elliot Ness."

Zelda bit her bruised lower lip, belted her robe around her midriff and trounced down a hall. She disappeared behind a door at the end. A moment later a radio began to play. First it was that damned Red Foley. She switched to Lawrence Welk interspersed with hog feed commercials. What a hell of a setting for cashing in; sow calls for a dirge and the living room furnished neatly enough for a PTA meeting.

Bogart crooked his fingers invitingly.

"Spill, Buddy."

"Spill what? I already gave you the story."

"Then take another book off the shelf. I don't like that first one."

Wiggling the muzzle of his cannon suggestively, Doug said, "Should we search him, boss?"

"Good idea. Go ahead."

He dropped into a flowered armchair, chomping his cigar while his uglies closed in. Doug grabbed. I slapped his hand, hard.

"Watch that stuff."

The hoodlum doubled up with laughter. "At least I gotta admire your guts. Go on, you guys. Shake him down. But let's be real gentle with him at first. If he cooperates, maybe we'll only maim him for life instead of killing him."

The apes performed the frisk with familiar ease. They dragged out wallet and lighter and motel key and other paraphernalia. All the loot was handed to the big man. He examined it piece by piece, then passed it to Lee Roy, who dropped the items in his pocket. Doug lounged near the fireplace, dangling his gun idly. Lee Roy walked in a circle, scratching his ugly dome as if hot on the trail of a peachy new way to murder me.

"Havoc." Bogart tented his fingers. "Name fits. You're causing me plenty."

"I'll cause a lot more if you don't let me walk out of here."

Annoyed, Bogart said, "Can it! Shall I lay out some facts for you, punk? Number one. You sure as hell weren't looking for Jones when you followed Judd Abel into the Glocca Morra."

I stuck out a finger. "So you admit you had him killed!"

Feigning innocence, he blinked rapidly. "Abel? Don't be silly."

"But you just said—"

He sighed. "Because I happen to know you were in a bar with another guy, that's evidence I had him killed? I saw all the details in the paper." He elevated his eyebrows and looked sanctified. "Judd Abel was a pal. A golf partner. But I'm doing the asking, remember? What do you want in this house?"

Maybe I had him running slightly hard. "The same thing you do."

He came out of the chair like an Atlas off the pad. "What's that mean?"

"Anything you want it to mean, Machiaveli."

Doug leveled his heater. "Don't go using them dirty foreign words on the boss."

"Ah, for God's sake! Bogart, how can we make a deal if these refugees from a Ziv show keep interrupting?"

"*Deal!*" Bogart wrenched my overalls awry again. "I

make no deals with punks. Tell me what you want here, dammit, and tell me quick."

I tried to ignore the cold knots in my gut, as well as his ugly puss. "Go fry. If that's not plain enough—" I repeated the message in Anglo-Saxon.

Shuddering wrathfully, Bogart called his punks: "Work on him. Nobody uses that language on me."

"Before they start, you'd better find out what I know about—"

*Splat.* He wasn't interested.

I dropped on all fours, my head lighting up from ear to ear. Doug prepared to bounce the cannon off my brains a second time. Bogart's laugh was cruel and tinny. I grabbed Doug's calf, yanked hard. He nearly went off balance. Nearly wasn't good enough. Bogart extended his leg and ground his heel on my knuckles.

"Hold your head up, midget!"

That was Doug, wrapping one hand around my skull to bring my chin in line with the cannon slashing down across his shoulder. I rammed a punch for his belly. It never connected.

Doug spilled over on his side, gabbing frantically. He came up in a crouch, muzzle swinging this way and that. When he saw who'd upset him he went pale:

"You clumsy bastard, Lee Roy—!"

"Ease off! I want to talk to the boss."

*"Ease off!"* howled Bogart, impotent with rage. "I'll ease off on you, jerk, if you try anything else like— huh? What's wrong? What's with all the motioning?"

"In the kitchen, for Crissake! I got an idea."

Bogart blinked. "Idea? Your last idea netted you fourteen months for robbing that goddamn pizzeria."

Smiling fit to be tied, Lee Roy couldn't be daunted. "Will you please come here just one second, boss? This is real important. You'll like it, I know you will."

"Well—" Bogart nodded at Doug. "If he escapes, so will you. On golden wings."

The unpleasant wretch and his hireling vanished. I sprawled on the carpet, wondering if Doug would lambast me if I got up. He didn't. I crawled to a chair, tried to listen to what was being said in the other room. Wayne King on the radio in the bedroom obscured things with that damned three-quarter time. I caught only an occasional furtive whisper from Lee Roy and cryptic comments from Bogart on the order of "Yeah?" and, "Show me." Then Bogart laughed and laughed.

Lee Roy swaggered back to the living room and regarded me with gooey pity. He indicated Doug's roscoe.

"Pass it to Mr. Bogart."

"Yeah, sure, I'll be gla—are you nuts? I haven't had fun like this in weeks."

"You'll have plenty of fun where you're going," said Bogart. "A chuckle a minute."

Deftly Bogart snatched the armament from his thug's pinkies. Lee Roy gave his companion a nudge. A moment later both walked out the front door.

A moment after that the Imperial took off in a snarl of cylinders. I retracted my jawbone from where it had fallen, down in the vicinity of the carpet.

"Did you get religion?"

"Don't be silly," Bogart dropped back to the flowered chair, resting his massive deterrent across his crooked knee. "I sent the gang out for some Danish. Think I can't handle a wart your size?"

Sweat funneled out of my pores like water over Niagara as I tried to decipher this latest move. I must have showed my utter bafflement.

"Don't look like somebody just gave you a hernia, Havoc. It's plenty simple. I decided you really aren't much of a pest after all. We'll have a nice chat. Then you go on about your seedy business." He bellowed with laughter.

For a second I gave long, hard thought to the swift change in the wind. Maybe it boiled down to Lee Roy having more sense than I gave him credit for. He might have talked the big cheese into avoiding the inevitable mess of another murder. But that didn't make much sense.

Then what could it be?

I didn't press the question too hard, grateful for the breath still whistling out of my undersized lungs. The ache in my head receded to mere torture. Was Bogart waiting for a hook to be dropped into his tough mouth? What did I have to lose?

"Bogart, I happen to know more about this piece of property than you think."

He was flat-faced, emotionless. "Is that so?"

I flung a leg over the arm of the chair. "When your thugs gave Abel his last golf lesson, all they did was knock me out. That was a mistake, considering what I learned from Ned Jones and various other people later."

That rocked him slightly, and he pinched his eyebrows together.

"What other people?"

"Never mind. You know I'm in a jam with the cops—"

"I heard something about a riot over on Seneca Circle. Was that you?"

"It wasn't Bullwinkle Moose, pal. I've gone to lots of trouble to slice this pie into a sufficient number of pieces to allow yours truly to have a hunk."

I couldn't quite be sure whether he was amused or panicky.

"What are you, Havoc? Not a private dick. There was no license in your wallet."

I shrugged. "A hustler."

He nodded. "Figures. There's a foxy look in your eye right this minute. Allow me to clear up one tiny detail. You keep referring to Abel and a golf lesson. I read about the poor guy being smashed with an iron all right. But I had nothing to do with it, absolutely nothing. Try to prove I did."

"Why should I? I'm on your side."

"Both of us behind bars, huh? You're a regular Bobbie Newhart, hustler."

"I'm serious!" I was on my feet. Histrionics could make or break the interview. I ignored the maw of the cannon on his knee and flapped my hands for emphasis: "I'm on the wrong end of the law just like you. What the hell do you suppose would happen if the sheriff got his hooks into me now?"

"Dunno," Bogart returned reflectively. "Since you're doing the blabbering, you tell me."

"I'd be socked away on a dozen charges. Dammit Bogart, let's not fence. Neither of us has clean hands. I know Judd Abel tried to slice the pie his way too. Deny it all day if you want to. It's still a fact that he was careless. He didn't put away insurance somewhere else besides in his head. Insurance to guarantee he wouldn't be killed. So he was."

"I got two words that blow your whole story to hell," Bogart purred. "Ham Anderson."

"Ham—" I felt like I'd swallowed a load of fast-curing concrete. "That—uh—was a mistake. I roughed him up before I thought about talking to you. It wasn't until a minute ago that I realized you were a right guy. Sensible. Willing to deal. Aren't you?"

Bogart scratched his chin, then his hard belly. Wayne King continued to assault the living room with mellifluous tones. A car stopped somewhere.

"In my considered opinion—" He grinned abruptly. "Ballsarooney."

"Okay, Bogart, okay! Play it cozy. But don't forget I may have my own collection of high cards. For instance, I happen to know exactly what kind of loot you're hiding down in the basement."

A completely wild stab based on Zelda's concern over the cellar blasted him between the eyes, squeezed a dot of perspiration onto his brow. While he was still groggy I let him have it again: "What's more, I know your name isn't Bogart. I have this friend. A guy named Underwood who works on the *Daily Times* in the city. I called him and he told me—"

Bogart was up again, digging an excavation in my belly with the gunsight.

"Told you what?"

I studied my fingernails blandly. "Enough."

He opened his mouth to challenge me, clamped it closed

again. His eyes grew dark, unreadable. I contemplated seizing the rod and cracking him in the head. My greed won out. This close to the green fountainhead, I couldn't resist. I should have.

"Now, Bogart, if you'll stop behaving like a comic book menace and listen to reason."

Like a toy on a spring his head snapped up.

"The door!"

With a disgusted sigh I watched him rush past. Doug and Lee Roy had undoubtedly returned. Bogart ripped the door open, thrusting the cannon into his back pocket at the same time.

I glanced idly at exit. Then not so idly. A dewlapped type in a union suit was capering up and down. He was accompanied by a number in a Sam Browne.

Officer Simms.

Bogart opened the screen part way. "Yeah, officer, what can I do for you?"

"Simms, Sheriff's department. Looking for a party who swiped this man's truck and clothes. The truck is at your curb but the man—"

"There he is! Oh Nelly, there he is!" screeched the dewlapped daddy, spotting me.

Instantly Bogart whipped out the cannon. Simms reached for his too.

"Glad you came officer, my God am I glad!" It was a perfect imitation of the terrified citizen. "This man broke in, tried to rob me. I've been holding him at bay with this ro—this empty gun I keep in my bureau."

Simms leveled his mammoth weapon, menacing me with the antisocial end. At the curb directly behind the Guernsey-Good wagon was his car, the motor still purring, the red light spinning round and round. Simms' eyes were about as full of the desire for blood vengeance as the law allowed.

Bogart kept talking at freight-train speed: "Every time I reached for the telephone, this crazy man threatened to jump me. I've been absolutely terrified. Take him away before he injures somebody."

Simms fastened his paw on my arm. "Come along, you. Sheriff Peel has a list of offenses that'll take a week to read."

I pointed to Bogart. "Arrest that man! He's the murderer of—"

"Not even loaded!" cried Bogart, waving his cannon. "Imagine that, officer!"

"Pretty brave of you, all right," said Simms, hustling me out the door while the dewlapped dairyman did a jig on the stoop and assorted suburbanites turned out of nearby houses to observe the quaint scene. "I'll send another man back for your statement about what happened, Mister—"

"Bogart, Edgar Bogart."

"Well, thanks, Mr. Bogart." Simms propelled me ahead violently. I shouted all sorts of protests. Not one penetrated. The mad minion of the law was bent on delivering me to Sheriff Peel's wringer. Once caught in it, I'd have no chance to clear myself. The situation was worse than desperate, it was hysterical.

I deigned a stumble, caught myself on Simms' arm. He rapped my knuckles with the heater.

"No tricks, Havoc. You're in too deep already."

"For God's sake let me get out of these overalls. I can barely walk. Besides, it's indecent, the way that milkman is standing around in his underwear."

"He's right," agreed Dewey. "I feel degenerate or something."

Simms backed off. Bogart was still smirking at the front door. I made a considerable show of stepping out of the big job. I held out the garment as Dewlaps reached.

I delivered the overalls smack into Simms' puss with a fast pitch. Then I pelted for the milk truck.

Kicking over the motor, I worked the floor stick and lit out down Mohawk Trail doing sixty.

# Chapter Ten

THE GEARS OF OLD Guernsey-Good groaned in protest as I adjusted my meager frame in the bucket seat. The seat was so high I nearly ripped all my ligaments stomping on the gas pedal.

From the side mirror I had a last appealing view of Officer Simms waltzing around Bogart's lawn in the embrace of the overalls. No time to stare further. I was an obvious quarry in a too-obvious bus.

A horn yowled. Out of a driveway dead ahead backed a Country Squire crammed with male golfers. I wrenched the wheel over. The moo van's bumper clipped the plastic tail light of the Squire. Then I was by, barreling around a snaky turn in Mohawk Trail onto a scenic stretch of housing development known as Iroquois Curve.

It was a curve, all right. It curved right back on itself in a swell dead-end oval.

I rammed the wheel all the way left. Milk bottles crashed in the rear racks. As I circled the oval Simms' car turned into Iroquois, siren blatting to beat hell.

Doors popped open everywhere. For a morning hour there seemed to be a high population of males attired in sport shirts. One of them, the nitwit, ran out in front of me, flailing his arms like a hero.

"Oh, murder," I groaned. "Not the Nathan Hale bit." I leaned on the horn.

Suddenly the householder got a clear look at my rapidly advancing grille. He thought better of his rashness and toppled butt over Bermudas into the parkway crabgrass. Other problems besieged me, namely Simms' buggy which was running as fast as mine on a head-on course.

The dumb nut fully intended to batter my few brains

90

out in a crash. I had nothing against any of the occupants of Iroquois Curve, but one of them was going to have to suffer. It happened to be the one with lengths of green lawn sprinkler coiled back and forth over his patch of sod. I cramped my molars together and veered the wheel.

The truck bounded up the parkway and over the sprinklers. Simms' car shot past, braking ferociously. One more bump that creamed my spleen and I was back on the asphalt, turning right back along Mohawk.

Officer Simms backed around in the street. The owner of the sprinkler scooped up several sections of the outraged plastic and dashed into Simms' path, vengefully hurling the damp segments through the open prowl car window. Simms leaned out. Even at my speed and distance his purple coloration was unmistakable. A house cut off the view.

Up the block the unfortunate Squire saw me coming again. The driver, half into the street, panicked and accidentally leaned on the gas. There was a horrible crash. The golfers had shot up the drive and demolished the door of an attached garage.

I hoped they had insurance and roared on toward the freeway and the bridge under which the road snaked its way back to Sylvan. Behind me, Simms was tooling fast, siren alive.

I couldn't hope to elude him for long with all the horses at his disposal under the hood of a souped-up police job. Watching the mirror, I shot under the express highway. Why was there such heavy traffic overhead? Then it registered—today was the start of the long Fourth of July weekend. Everyone was home.

Cancel that. Half were home and half were on the road, the latter half being women en route to the shopping plaza to load up the larder. Traffic whizzed both ways. Simms' siren shrilled imperiously. But you know how much ice anything like that cuts with a woman driver.

I searched for a way out of the General Motorized Tangle. A front tire of the milk boat struck a pothole, blew out with a crack.

It took all my failing nerve and strength to hang on to the whipsawing vehicle. When it was under control, I flung out my left arm and turned left in front of a Jag.

The suburban lovely in the sport job whammed her pedal. All her groceries skyrocketed from sacks in the seat beside her. Loaves of bread, cans of corn and jars of peanut butter flew every which way as I rammed down a lane in the plaza parking lot. There was such a profusion of busted peanut butter jars on the highway that traffic came to a standstill.

I looked for a spot to park the Guernsey-Good van before the blown tire upset everything, aced into a diagonal and leaped out, snatching my jacket and porkpie which I'd been shrewd enough to leave on the floor after donning the overalls. Just as my soles hit the pavement I saw Simms shove the prowl car into the plaza across the low guard strip that separated highway from parking lot. He'd been too impatient to wait for the peanut butter traffic jam, with its caterwauling horns and sobbing females. The prowl car was keening straight toward me. I ducked for the shops along the plaza arcade.

The walks were jammed. A hand clutched my sleeve.

"Mister, donation please?"

I smacked into a female tank with a fifty-inch bosom and a lavender overseas cap. She jangled a tin can under my nose.

"Donation for the Ladies' Auxiliary of the Veterans of the War of 1812?"

"Leggo, lady. There can't be any veterans of 1812 anymore."

"Is that any way to talk about charity?"

She refused to unclutch. Already Simms was out of his heap, boots hammering as he ran.

"Is that any way for this man to talk about charity, folks? Look at him all dressed up in a fancy suit, living it up in an affluent society while the world goes to hell—"

I gave her a poke in her affluent ribs.

"Masher! Sex maniac!"

But her hands were no longer leeching. I ran through

the nearest glass door, planning to dodge out the back way into the woods that edged the plaza, when perfume assailed me. A woman gabbled.

I bumped against a broad's chest.

"Pardon me. Oh my God."

The chest was solid pine and the cutie smiled a vacant mannequin's smile. Shrill female screams rose up all around. Backways through plate glass I read the bad news. *Salon de Paris, Sophisticated Creations Exclusively For Madame.*

"Young man, you can't come in here, this is only for—"

But Simms was on the way, cannon up and face the hue of plums. I raced around the old bat and ran for the back. I would have been safer in a pit of asps.

Another female accosted me between hats and nighties. She pushed and pushed. Nearly five-ten, the broad held me like a line-blocker. A pneumatic door stopper shooshed. Official-type boots crashed on tile. The manageress or whatever the hell she was stared over my head, lamped Simms' cannon and prepared to drop her upper plate in surprise. I quickly denuded a mannequin and wrapped a nightie of a shade called Hot Blush around her head.

The bag hopped about like Cyd Charisse with a case of hives. Simms bawled, "That's enough, you little punk. Turn around before I have to blast—"

I up-ended the wooden cutie and heaved her through the air.

Simms saw her coming, tried in vain to dodge, and digested five wooden fingers. I hit the hat counter with my palm, vaulted over and trundled fast as my sawed-off legs would carry me toward a satin curtain in the wall bisecting the store. Last thing I saw, the manageress had fallen on top of Simms and both of them were sharing the intimacy of yards and yards of Hot Blush.

Congratulating myself on my clever escape, I bolted through the curtain into the stock room. I discovered it wasn't the stockroom as soon as a dozen old broads started screaming.

A model on a raised platform tried to cover up her foundation garment, which had more hasps, buckles, claws and prongs than a motorcycle jacket.

"Lady, lady, you're stepping on my *eeeyow!*" shrieked Simms somewhere.

"No men allowed!" This was another store female, rising from a chair. The dames in the audience, not a one of them weighing less than two hundred, screamed like they really had some goodies worth going after. The screams brought two other models scampering from behind another curtain. They were attired in not much of anything in the way of black lace.

I lowered my head and cut for that escape hatch.

"It's a rapist, a rapist, my God, we'll all be attacked!"

Instead of more screams there were a few giggles. I dashed madly past the dais. The model had more presence of mind than the rest. She snatched my shoulder.

"You can't disrupt our showing this way! Miss Fretchie, for God's sake help me hold him! Who's that shouting?"

"Police, police!" rang strangled Simms' cry. "Lady, please, watch out for that spiked heel, you already gave it to me once in the ohboyoh*boy!*"

The model number, bony and tough as a bargain steak, began gouging me with her elbows. Being models' elbows, they had as much flesh on them as the end of a carving knife. Miss Fretchie ran here and there opining at the top of her lungs that she guessed the man in front was from the police.

The model snarled and bit and clawed. Soon as I pried off one of her hands, three more took its place. Lace bashed me in the chops. One of the broads in the audience climbed up on a chair as though someone had unloosed a mouse. I screwed my head around just as Simms dove through the curtain.

My hand accidentally hooked something metallic. Trying to give me a past, the model knocked me off balance.

That's how I happened to unzip her foundation from the cleavege down.

Next thing I knew, I was holding the contraption by the zipper while Simms struggled through the bags hovering around him for protection. The model was fainting from the shame of nudity and I was waving the garment like a battle flag.

"Watch out, watch out!" shrilled Simms. "That man's dangerous. Somebody seize him."

None of the biddies was about to try. But the models weren't so retiring. They stormed at me. I dropped on all fours, scuttled between four charming calves and danced through the second curtain.

Somebody hit me in the dark hallway. Cursing, I lit into the attacker with both fists. When I recovered my senses, I saw I'd scored a knockout on a wire dress form. It was spinning its wheels in defeat.

Simms ripped the curtain clean off its rings and shouted, "Hands up!" or some other nonsense.

"Care to dance?" cried I, rolling the dress form along the floor at top speed.

Simms couldn't plug me through that hurtling wire cage. It bounced him back into the salon where he and it executed a step vaguely resembling the twist.

I ran for the rear door. Several additional forms stood in a row near the entrance. I overturned them one after another to form an impromptu barricade. Then I popped into the sunlight, blinking. What I needed now was a way to throw Simms off the track for good.

Yanking off my porkpie, I scaled it through the air, watched it settle in the weeds at the fringe of the trees near a path.

A semi-trailer parked to the left attracted my attention to the loading dock of the Great Atlantic & Pacific food emporium. This side of the truck, I noticed some tall restaurant refuse cans. Pint size does have its occasional advantages. In five seconds I was inside, up to my pelvis in squishy malted milk cups, my scalp pressed tight against the galvanized lid. I felt like an inmate of a medieval torture chamber. I had Hershey's chocolate all over my brogans. But it was slightly better than jail.

Simms' hollering came tinnily through the can walls, then grew fainter. I risked inching up the lid a fraction, saw the cop dart toward the woods, heft my porkpie, swivel his head like a turret, then take off down the path into the forest where Judd Abel had gotten his.

A bus boy from the restaurant was depositing a case of Pepsi empties on the cement. "Jeez, who left that thing open?" I felt the whack of the lid from my dome down to my bunions.

Thirty minutes was the limit of my endurance. To hell with Simms. I lifted the lid and stepped out. A guy unloading crates on the semi turned pale and dropped a crate on his toe. I smiled winningly as I sponged a gob of banana split off my pants and hotfooted for the trees.

"Smirtnik, Smirtnik! Guess what! I just saw a guy come out of that garbage can."

"Quiet, quiet! Want to get fired for hitting the sauce! So maybe the housing shortage is worse around here than we figured."

In a mossy patch beneath a generous briar bush, I flopped down, stoked up a weed and caught my breath. Birds racketed in overhead bougias as if no one had a care in the world. My head ached. My stomach was empty. My prospects were rotten.

A clatter arose not six feet away. I lay like one embalmed, catching a glimpse of polished boots gallumping from path to paved area behind the stores. It was Simms, cannon in one hand, porkpie in the other. The semi had disappeared from behind the Great Atlantic & Pacific, sparing me the embarrassment of discovery for a few more moments.

Simms scratched his head. He glanced around in the sunlight, the picture of perplexity and rage.

Then he lammed off around the corner of the building, no doubt to phone for assistance.

I headed deeper into Willoughby's Woods, marching for

half a mile up hill and down dale till I discovered a cozy hollow in the side of an embankment. It was filled with termites and other pleasant little beasties. I whiled away the morning hours there, stiff, chilly, hungry as a Russian general at the Finnish border. Along toward noon Simms returned with the troops.

They crashed this way and that through the woods, hallooing to one another in official tones. But the brush was so thick they hadn't a prayer of discovering me, especially since I had decorated the entrance of the little hollow with branches and other woodsy stuff. At last they retreated. The sun moved with impossible slowness down toward the western horizon and the hours of dark when I'd be free to operate.

How much time did I have? I guessed one more night would be it. Thus far I'd had a run of luck that would have driven a Vegas pit boss out on his skull. A rough plan had suggested itself between sessions of studying the termites marching here and there over my person looking for edibles.

When the shadows finally lengthened I crawled out of my hole. I slogged back to the plaza. It was slightly past six. All the stores had shuttered up tight in preparation for the Fourth tomorrow. Only the short-order restaurant was open.

I sidled inside, had a quick burger and three cups of metallic coffee, then hit the phone booth in the rear.

"*Daily Times* in the city; Will Underwood. Collect. The name is Lutz."

"I wish I'd never heard of gin rummy," Will complained when I got him. "Or you either."

"Come on, Pulitzer, make it snappy. Things are popping out here. I may be hauled to the Bastille any sec."

"I should guess so. You're turning into a regular Dr. Crippen."

His meaning blissfully eluded me. "What about Bogart?"

"I wasted my lunch hour, but I found it. Nearly fifteen

years back. Luckily our morgue man is a pretty clever old geezer. He remembered. He dug up the right file the minute I said Bogart. Got to put in a good word for old Hemmelfinger, he's really sharp."

"Spare me the employee relations and give me the facts."

"The real cognomen of your friend is Bogardus." He hesitated suggestively. "Mean anything?"

"Hang on, hang on!" Little wheels clicked. "Emile! That it?"

"Better known as Banjo. Banjo Bogardus the heist artist."

I snapped my fingers. Pieces fell into place. "Where was it? A foundry!"

"Close. Rumsdale Iron Works. Payroll amounting to two hundred and fifty grand."

"Hell, I was practically a teen-ager." I grinned in spite of my weariness. I could practically smell the green ink in George Washington's wig. "Wasn't there a splashy trial?"

"You bet there was. And a fast trip to the pen for Banjo. He tried to escape three months after they whacked him inside. He hid out in the city for a week under the Bogart alias. That's what clued old Hemmelfinger. Bogardus was released early this year. Turned into a model prisoner after he was clapped in the second time. The release is the last item in our file."

I headed the receiver for the prongs. "Thanks, Will. We'll play gin again soon as—"

"My God, hold it!"

He lowered his tone to a whisper that iced my spine: "Listen, I expect a story from you, Johnny. A break for the *Times* on the two sensational Sylvan slayings the police think were perpetrated by a city boy named Ha— Are you calling from a men's room? You sound like you're gargling."

"Will," I said tightly, "I thought I heard you used the number two in connection with homicide."

"Sure. It's smeared all over the front of the *Times* tonight."

I tried to swallow the cannonball in my windpipe. "I only know of one dead body."

Will groaned. "What about the corpse in the—wait. Here it is. The E-Z-Doz Motel. We've had it since three. Body discovered in a room belonging to a Mr. Lutz. Skull caved in."

I remained speechless. Presently he went on: "The sheriff of that burg out there has even identified Mr. Lutz from a description he got from a maid. Listen, Johnny, what's up? They've got you pegged. Your name is in our subhead. You're hot, man."

"Thanks for the name bit in the head. Thanks a hell of a lot."

"Dammit, I wasn't on the desk then. I didn't write it. If I were you—"

"You wouldn't like being me, Will. It's pretty discouraging. Did they identify the body?"

"Anderson," he said grimly. "A tavern owner named Ham Anderson."

# Chapter Eleven

AFTER LAME THANKS I hung up. In the next minute I came close to tossing out the scheme I'd concocted while holed up in the woods. I didn't, though. With two dead numbers chalked up against me, it was more important than ever that I hoist the chestnuts from the fire with all possible speed. The nasty pattern was shaping up fast.

Bogart—no, it was Banjo Bogardus; I kept forgetting —must have ordered his cretins to hand Anderson his lumps for bungling my kill in the basement of the Glocca Morra. Anderson was plainly an unstable type. What was one more closed mouth to a professional like Banjo? I tried to round out an explanation of Bogart's nutty behavior at his house that morning.

As far as I could dope it, the uglies must have been carrying Anderson's body in the Imperial trunk. In a cold sweat I remembered Lee Roy examining my things, among which was an embossed key for my room at the E-Z-Doz Motel. That must have given him the big flash. No wonder Bogardus had tittered like a loony during the whispering fest. And practically written me off after his goons barreled away to plant the corpse.

Sweating by the gallon, I used my last pants-pocket bill to collect a buck's worth of change from the restaurant cashier, who lamped the chocolate stains on my slacks with ill-concealed curiosity. In the directory I checked out the name Porter, Stan P. Presently a maple-syrup man's voice answered.

"Hullo, this is Porter."

I debated challenging him right over the wire, decided against it.

"Is your daughter home?"

"Who wants her, may I ask?" He inquired officiously.

"Tell her it's Percy Hamilton. I'm an old friend."

His oozing voice shouted Winnie's name away from the mouthpiece. I passed the time by guessing how long I'd be sentenced to prison if they caught me. Ten years? Fifteen? A lifetime? Maybe I could make some bucks writing a book about life inside the pen. Even behind bars there must be ways to pick up a few—

"Percy Hamilton? I'm afraid I don't know you, Mr. Hamilton. This isn't a sales call, is it? We don't want any aluminum awnings."

"How about midgets under your bed?" I whispered. "In the market?"

"Oh!" Her gasp was startled. "Oh, my goodness!"

"Careful! Don't mention my name."

"Why—why, no. I saw the local paper this afternoon and—just a second. There. Stan's gone back to the living room. Honestly, I don't think I should trust you, Jo— Percy, after that gruesome account of what the police found in the motel. It was your room, wasn't it?"

"Of course it was," I growled. "But I didn't cool him. The Bogart bunch did. And his name's not Bogart, it's Banjo Bogardus. He's a pro with a record three times as long as my whole body. Winnie, I don't blame you for smelling stale fish, but I swear I can straighten things out with your help."

"What do I have to do? Help hide bodies?"

"For God's sake not so loud! Bring your car to the shopping plaza on the Olympus Acres road. Pick me up in front of the Acropolis Fancy Short Order Grille. Know where that is? Good. I'd walk, but if I'm spotted I'll never have a chance to clear myself. I need you, Winnie. It's the only way."

Hesitation.

"I'm not sure whether I ought to. So much violence—"

"A couple of hours and it'll be wrapped up," I promised. "Don't forget, there aren't many people in the world our size. It's sort of like a lodge. All for one and one—"

"—on the lookout for bales of money," she cut me off. "All right. I'll be there soon."

She hung up. I tottered back to the counter to wash down my trepidation with more coffee. Before long, headlights flashed across the glass front. A few seconds later I was riding beside her out of the plaza lot.

"Drive back to your neck of the woods," I said. "The number who can unstick this sticky mess is Stan P. Porter. Gotta see him, tonight. I hope he's still home."

"Still there. But Johnny, you won't hurt him? Or do anything violent? Will you?"

I patted her hand where it rested on the wheel and experienced a series of delightful hormonal nip-ups.

"How big is Stan P., hon?"

"Nearly six feet. He weighs almost two hundred."

"Then you can count on the mayhem being strictly mental. I don't want the old boy burned. Because of you. Besides, I have a feeling he wasn't responsible for the deaths. Somehow he's on the sidelines, maybe coaching the team on a few of the trick plays, but I tag Bogardus and his helpers for the homicide bit. All I want from Stan P. is suggestions about the nature of the caper he and the crooks are mixed up in. From that point on, I surrender my carcass to the bulls and hope to God Banjo's record will take the onus off me. This whole dizzy play is becoming just too damned complicated." I sighed. "Hope there's a reward for whatever Banjo's after in the—wait a minute!"

I sat up so suddenly I startled her. She was turning into a side street. She hit the brake at my outcry, causing my dome to contact the dash. Next thing I knew, she was bending over me, murmuring get-well sentiments:

"Did I hurt you, Johnny? I didn't mean to stop so fast."

I was within inches of her face. It seemed only logical to go the whole route. She didn't seem to mind.

Her lips responded, parting, sending juice at a few million volts a second up and down my quivering nerves.

I clutched her around the middle, plus several other places. We were up to our necks in darkness, the only light was one of those globe streetlamps at the block's end. Winnie's copper hair was warm against my cheek.

Her hands grew slightly eager. With a dismal sigh I eased her away.

"Better not. Else I'll neglect Stan P. and try to make the scene a statistic in one of those suburban sex reports. You're a distracting wench, y'know."

"And you make me glad, Johnny, for the first time in a long time, that I'm only five feet."

She poked the end of my ugly nose giddily.

"They'd better not send you to jail. I've got plans for you. When you invaded my bedroom, I was outraged. Until I thought it over. I decided you're nice. I can be nice too, to the right guy."

"Bet you can," I mumbled. "Better drive on before I weaken."

Regretfully she flipped the stick, eased the car down the darkened street in the direction of Stan P.'s castle, saying, "But your head—I really didn't mean to pull up so sharply. You shouted as though you'd been stung by a bee."

"I was. A bee with a two hundred and fifty grand price tag. Pull over."

Puzzled, she obeyed, parked in the shadows between two of the lights. The Porter residence was a full block away.

"I thought you wanted to talk to Stan."

I opened the door, climbed out.

"I do. But alone. Wait here. I don't plan to be more than half an hour. I'm sure Stan will play my way."

I grinned down at her, failing on purpose to mention how I intended to make him join the game. But I couldn't resist leaning across one more time and bussing those luscious lips. We managed to get tangled for the better part of five minutes. Finally I answered duty's feeble call.

"Soon as I'm back I'll go face Peel and company. But if Stan's mixed up in murder—"

"Johnny, a human life isn't exactly a sack of popcorn. Even if Stan were my own flesh and blood I'd have to prepare myself for his taking what's coming." She patted me on the cheek and flashed me a smile. "Just be careful. As I said, I have plans for that five-foot-one physique."

In a renewed mood, I walked down the street, through the gate and up to the Charles Addams pad she and pops inhabited. I made noises at the front door. After a moment Stan P. heaved his bulk into sight, opening the door a crack.

"What do you want?" His maple-syrup voice had soured somewhat.

"Evening, Porter. Move back."

I tried to look tough as I insinuated myself through the door. Attired in slacks, oxblood brogans and a white shirt whose monogram was as frayed as his reputation, Stan P. beetled at me as I slammed the portal with my rump, folded my arms and regarded him in an unfriendly manner. He was bald, pasty-cheeked; the relic of a man who had once eaten high off the hog. These days he was obviously chewing the knuckles.

"The name is Havoc. Where can we talk?"

"I don't know you or the name—"

Suddenly his face resembled an unwashed blackboard. He lifted a porky paw which clutched the latest example of Sylvan yellow journalism. I glimpsed my name prominently displayed. He shuffled back a step, two. He had amateur crook written all over his greedy puss, but I reminded myself to be careful of the mean glitter in his small eyes.

"You're the one! The body in the motel room!"

He lunged like a mastodon for the rear of the house.

"Hold it, beefy, if you want to see Winnie again. I travel under several aliases. One is Percy Hamilton."

"Goddamn you!"

His fingers hunted my neck. I started away, laughed in his face. His jowls sagged. He licked his lips.

"You're bluffing, Havoc."

"Try finding her, fatty. You'll see whether I'm bluffing or not."

"What have you done with Winnie?"

"Put her in a safe spot. No harm will come to her unless I go away from here minus what I want. Namely, a condensed account of the hijinks you and Emil Bogardus are involved in."

He feigned stupidity. "Bogardus? Who's Bogardus?"

"Dammit, Porter, quit the Actor's Studio bit. Either play along or I'll get the hell out of here. And go see your Winnie," I finished with a snarl.

His fingers committed mayhem on the paper. "I ought to break you apart."

"Blubber, I'd be out of here so quick you'd be left at the starting line."

I gestured to a door opening on one of the three sitting rooms. A modern lamp burned on a teak coffee table, its beam lighting up the sweat of his jowls. I had him by the privates and he knew it.

"Let's get down to business, Porter."

All at once he appeared to melt like butter in the sun. He dragged out a brow-mopper and mopped.

"Okay, okay. God, I don't want any harm to come to Winnie. I'm sick of the whole mess anyway. I never intended that there should be killing."

I couldn't be sure whether he was stalling, but I took a chance he wasn't. He followed me into the sitting room.

"What about a drink, Havoc? We can discuss this more easily with a drink."

He wrung his hands. It had been easier than I thought. I had him cold.

"Winnie's safety means a lot to me, Havoc. I'll cooperate. What do you want to drink?"

"Pour me a belt of rye. Make it a double, no ice."

"I have to go to the kichen—"

"Do that, Stan. If you come back with a cleaver, or if

you don't come back at all, I hope you'll rest easy over what happens to Winnie."

I gave him my most loathsome smirk. I felt somewhat loathsome myself, using her as lever. But hadn't she told me her stepfather had to square up if he was embroiled in homicide?

Porter responded to the bluff with gargled promises that he'd try no tricks. His lardy backside waddled out of sight. I cocked an ear, heard a tinkle of glassware and the rush of tap water. Another couple of minutes, the tap was shut off and Porter was back, pressing a glass on me. He drained his highball with one greedy gulp.

"Shall I commence with a few pregnant facts, Porter?" I inquired. "First, I know you're part of the scheme that ramrodded Ned Jones out of his place on Mohawk Trail. Your ex-foreman Abel mentioned your name in conjunction with the plot the night Banjo's playmates let Judd have it. So don't bother denying every step."

His guilty squint told me all I wanted to know. If he hadn't attended the first kill, he wasn't ignorant of who had done it, either.

"I have a sneaky suspicion about what's in that house, Stan. I want you to confirm it for me." I leered over the rim of the rye. "Ever hear of the Rumsdale Iron Works?"

Porter's chops flopped open. He collapsed against the wall.

"My God, how did you know about that?"

"I didn't, until tonight. You sing the next verse chum. From the top."

Porter passed a damp hand across his brow, "All right. You know who Bogart is. You apparently know about the Rumsdale Iron Works robbery. Two hundred and fifty thousand dollars free and clear. Bogardus went to prison for the job. But he told the prosecutor the loot had been split up between some of his cronies who weren't caught, said they'd taken off for Mexico and Brazil. No one could prove him wrong."

"And Bogardus had the greenies stashed all the time?"

He nodded. Droplets of sweat rivered down to his collar. Suddenly he laughed. I didn't like the laugh. All at once his words grew more confident. "See if you can figure the next step. I had a construction business. I took a section of land on the outskirts of Sylvan near the freeway—"

"Pretty condescending tone you're using, Stan lad."

"So what? I'm giving you answers. My bulldozers knocked down every tree on that pasture. I built Olympus Acres. Damned sound houses for the price in spite of —ah, forget it. Bogardus was finally released from prison."

"Hang on!" All the lights went up at once. "In your file there's a plat. Shut up, never mind how I found out about it. With a big red-crayoned X."

"Brainy little punk, aren't you? Well, you're right. That's where Bogardus buried the money. Out in the country that wasn't the country when he was free again. The northeast quadrant of Dado's Pasture, Block 99. Bogardus looked me up right away."

Porter's expression grew unpleasant as he thought of all the bad plastering that had ruined him. "By that time I was ready to try anything. So I went in business with him."

"Worked out the location of the buried loot? Under the Jones house, correct?"

"You deserve a cash prize. What else do you want to know?"

"Abel's part. How come he was dished a helping of the dessert?"

Stan P. shrugged. "He did much of the original surveying. Besides, I thought he was strong for Winnie and some of the money would give them a start in life."

"Disinherited families and dead bodies. Swell wedding presents. Where did Bogardus get the cash to put up for Ned's place?"

"Twenty of the original thirty-five offered was Banjo's. The other fifteen was mine, every cent I had in the bank after lawsuits cleaned me out. Turned out that we didn't need it after all."

"Jones wouldn't sell so Bogardus and Ham Anderson arranged the phony fight and the accident?"

"That's right." Porter chuckled, a positively nasty sound. "I wonder why the devil I bother to tell you all this. Well, in any case murder wasn't included in the original plan. I've had nothing to do with any killings." A rush of scarlet filled his suet cheeks. "Except maybe yours."

Before I could express surprise, he sidled forward, rubbing his hands. "Head all full of facts now, Havoc? Your dirty hustler's tricks may work in the city, but they won't out here. I happen to know you're a free agent. It's all in the paper tonight. No detective agency connections, nothing like that. So you have Winnie hidden, do you? I haven't really been worried, except right at first. You'll tell me where she is the minute Doug and Lee Roy arrive."

"You overweight sneak!" I warned.

Once more the maple-thick tone of the star salesman, the housing con artist, greased his words: "Did you hear the tap water running when I mixed the drink? Thanks to that water, you undoubtedly *didn't* hear me talking to the operator. I phoned Banjo."

"Phoned—you goddamn idiot! Winnie's right outside in her car. Those goons are liable to go crazy!"

Panicked, Porter leaped to bar my path as I zipped for the front hall.

"Winnie *outside*?"

I pasted him hard in the guts.

Collapsing against the wall, Stan P. freed the exit. I made fast use of it, pummeling down the driveway to the street. It was deathly quiet.

Behind me I heard the bumbling contractor bellow and howl. I was only concerned about the lurched silhouette of Winnie's heap outlined against a distant lamp. Racing for it, I saw that two of the tires had been slashed, the windshield broken into crazy starred patterns.

I yanked open the right door. The car was empty.

"Where is she?" Stan P. moaned, rushing up. "Where's my daughter?"

"With your sweet friends," I said, madder than I'd been in a long time. "Some bunch, Porter. They've been here and gone. Must have spotted her in the car. God knows why they took her. And for cripe's sake stop blubbering! I ought to be shot for getting her into—what's that?"

"Why did they do it?" Porter sobbed. "I'm a partner."

I paid no attention, cold clear through when I picked up the item that had been partially hidden by the front seat: a very small pump, kicked off in what must have been a hell of a struggle.

Stan P. lumbered away and stood weeping against a light pole. I stared at the shoe and wondered dumbly what was going to happen next.

# Chapter Twelve

"THE COPS!"

To say it was about as pleasant as swallowing cyanide, but what choice was left?

"The cops, Porter. We have to telephone them. Don't stand there like a wounded whale."

I shoved him in the spine. He shuffled forward, muttering into his fat palms.

"That's it, the police. It can't be any other way." I said it mainly for my own benefit, having second thoughts about how trusting they'd be of my story. Porter stumbled up the darkened driveway ahead of me. Deep inside the house a phone rang.

I darted past him up the steps, crashed through a swinging door into the kitchen, tore off the receiver.

"Porter?" The growl was familiar. "Is this Porter?"

"No, he's coming, wait a—Bogardus! This is Havoc. Where's Winnie?"

A malicious chuckle assaulted my eardrum.

"Guess, fink. Leave me talk to the fat man."

"If you hurt that doll, Banjo, I swear—"

"You'll do what? Think unkind thoughts? Don't make me wet my shorts laughing. You got plenty to keep you busy with that dead body in the motel. And that stuff at the plaza today. You should tune in the radio once in a while, punk. Your antics are a scream."

"Bogardus, I demand to talk to Winnie—"

"Shut up! You're talking to nobody. Put Porter on and make it quick."

Trembling and puffing, Stan P. clutched the frame of the kitchen door like he was ready for thrombosis. I gestured frantically, jammed the receiver into his meaty

110

fingers. When he ground the earpiece against his head, I pried the plastic away from his lobe so I could get an earful too.

"Huh—hullo?"

"Stan? This is Banjo. We're dissolving the partnership, you doublecrossing sonofabitch."

The crumbling contractor moaned anew. "Banjo, what kind of talk is that? Didn't I call to let you know I needed help?"

"What were you trying to do?" sneered the hoodlum. "Rub my nose in it? Doug and Lee Roy got the message plenty clear—you and that city hustler with your heads together. I guess you thought if Abel tried to help himself to a fatter slice, you might as well do the same. Well, it won't work. My boys are smart. They spotted the broad in her car and she's here in the house right now."

"How could you possibly think I'd sell out? I didn't—"

"Not much you didn't," Bogardus snarled. "Lee Roy saw you through the curtain, smiling to beat hell while you opened your face to that little jerk."

"I was only stalling!"

"Frankly, fat ass, I don't much care either way. You're becoming a pain. You never had the guts for this caper in the first place. We'll be finished and out of here by dinner time tomorrow, maybe sooner. Until then, your Winnie keeps us company. Just remember I can chop her before the cops walk in. And I'll stay alive long enough to land you in prison."

"So you're selling me out, you rotten crook!"

"Buddy, I'm just returning the favor you did me with that Havoc jerk." Banjo laughed flatly again, and added, "He's having his clock stopped too. Doug and Lee Roy saw to it on the way back. Well, so long, Porter. Thanks for the plat anyway."

Porter clutched the phone with both hands. "But Banjo! I need my share of—"

"Doublecrossers deserve what they get. Which is zero. I said so long."

"I didn't have time to tell you over the phone Havoc was with me!" he screamed. "You're making a hideous mistake if you think—"

*Click, click.*

Stan P. no longer had an audience.

So sore I could have eaten penny nails, I slapped the phone from his fists. I crammed him up against the wall, reached up and chopped him in the cheeks. I gave him a few more just to vent my feelings.

"You greedy slug!"

*Chop, chop.*

"You miserable money-grubbing bum! I may be a hustler but by hell I wouldn't sell out my own step-daughter! I've half a mind to break your flabby neck."

Quavering, Porter ducked away from the barrage, the picture of utter misery.

"Don't hurt me, Havoc! Don't hurt me any more! I'm wiped out. Absolutely ruined. I staked everything on that man!"

I twisted his monogram a few times. "How about Winnie's life? Did you stake that too?"

"I lost my head, lost my head! You're clever. Think of something. Banjo's digging up the Jones cellar with an air hammer—"

I chewed my lip like gum and paced the kitchen. "I saw it this morning."

"He's dug a dozen holes or more. I couldn't give him the precise location of the money. He told me early today—we were rained out of the golf course—that he had only a few more square feet of concrete to turn over. The money has to be under it. If he says he'll be finished by tomorrow night, he means it. He's liable to *kill* Winnie before he leaves town. Havoc, *do* something!"

I kicked him in the shins.

"How can I think with you bellowing, you dumb ox?"

The phone receiver was conking the plaster, going round and round, crazily at the end of its kinked plastic cord. From the diaphragm issued a female voice:

"Hello, hello plizz? Who is using this phone? Hello, plizz?"

Fatty grabbed the instrument, masked the talk end with his palm while the operator continued to complain.

"Havoc, call the police!"

"And take a chance on Bogardus hurting Winnie? No soap, I'll think of another way."

"But if enough men stormed the house—"

"Hang up!" I did it for him. "Porter, when I talked about the cops I was out of my head. Besides what Banjo told us, there's the little matter of how I've screwed up the local force. How long would they listen if I fed them the story that a perfectly innocent girl is being held prisoner in a housing tract that's strictly from *Better Homes and Gardens*? They wouldn't believe me first because I'm me, second because things like this don't happen in such refined surroundings. And don't tell me everybody's *your* buddy down at city hall, either."

Stung, Porter sighed and wiped a crocodile tear.

"You're right. They've all been on my neck. Tax assessor, county judges, everybody."

Porter's face was an unhealthy gray under the ceiling fluorescents. I really couldn't tell whether he was motivated out of genuine concern for Winnie or a desire to see Banjo pay up for cutting off his water. It didn't matter a hell of a lot. I was rapidly going gaga listening to his complaints as I cut for the sitting room where I could hear myself do what passed for thinking, when a fresh burst of grief came bellowing out: "Oh, dammit, yes. Yes, nobody in uniform would lift a finger to help us."

"You can say that again. Nobody in uniform would—"

The experience resembled illuminating all the bumpers on a pinball after you've given the rig a stiff tilt. I spun in the kitchen door and threw a finger at Stan P.

"Stan baby, that's *it*! You're a genuis! For once in your miserable life you had an idea!"

His eyelids worked all in a spasm.

"I thought you said we couldn't appeal to—"

"Not that, not that. The uniform bit. Police uniforms, army uniforms, any old damn uniform. That's the secret to getting Winnie out of that rat's nest alive and unharmed. Wait till I tell Junior Jones! I'll show him Johnny Havoc knows a thing or two about books!"

There was an echo in the joint: "John Havoc, John Havoc."

And then the echo said, "We have you surrounded."

"Oh my God, my *God*." Stan P. sank down alongside the garbage disposal, which is exactly where he belonged. I bolted past him to the back porch, cursing the day Bell invented the talking box and Doug and Lee Roy learned how to use it. I didn't have much doubt about who put the law dogs on me.

I bagged onto the porch and whacked my shin on a piece of dusty lawn furniture. The stentorian voice on the bullhorn opened up again: "Havoc, we know you're in there. Better come out with hands raised. There are men all around the house. This is Buster Peel talking, Havoc. I warn you we're in no mood to go easy. Come out of there unless you want a whiff of tear gas."

I slid against the porch wall out of the light, wishing Stan P. would stop his yammer. It drew men to the dark rear of the house. Like a plastered Frankenstein, Porter hauled his flab into the doorway and hung there bellowing, "Don't shoot, officers! Havoc's here all right. I'll lock him on the porch so he can't get back inside."

While I cursed him with every unprintability I could think of, the louse did exactly that, leaping back into the kitchen, snapping the latch triumphantly. Boots clunked on wooden steps.

"We see you in there, mister. Come out with your hands high."

I feigned disillusionment, stepping into the glimmering gleam falling through the grimy plate glass of the kitchen door.

"All right, I surrender."

I shuffled toward the exit in a coward's stance. One of the law dogs, black jacket throwing off leathery highlights, opened the porch door. At the bottom of the four steps he stood with a companion, both with guns drawn. Another minion ran pell mell from the direction of the street, urging Sheriff Peel to rush to the site immediately.

Poised at the top of the four steps, I raised my hands over my nut.

"Very well, men. I'm all yours."

They got me, in a swan dive right on top of them. My own dead weight was sufficient to clobber them both. If their cannons went off, I was cooked, but I was in too deeply to worry much. My elbow caught one of them in the schnoozz, my knee jabbed the other one in the ribs. Both howled like they'd been emasculated. The three of us fell in a heap on the grass.

"For Crissake, Fritterham, get your heel out of my mouth before I—*glob*."

Struggling for his very life, Fritterham only succeeded in driving his tootsie further between his mate's molars. I gave him a taste of knuckles and he went to sleep. I leaped up and sat down. That took care of the one who had been globbing.

But more were on the way, including Sheriff Peel himself. His corpulence blocked out a distant street light. I snatched Fritterham's cap, jammed it on my head, blustered through the dark shadows next to the house. Sheriff Peel bumped me with his belly.

"Who is it? Have you got him?"

"Arbuthnot, sir," I saluted with the wrong hand. "He's tussling and struggling back there but I believe Fritterham has the situation under control."

"Good, good!" Peel accidentally whacked my head with his bullhorn as he ran off. I was thrown against the side of the house, the back of my skull contacting a sill with a loud, hard pop.

"Gotta get away," I mumbled. "Winnie. Uniforms. Oh, mother."

A collection of canaries between my ears was singing loudly. The crack of the sill was harder than I'd thought.

And some rat had substituted latex where my leg bones should have been.

I tottered a step. Out of the black came Peel's shout: "Arbuthnot? There's no Arbuthnot on the—*stop that man!*"

"Try it!" I gargled to the first sheriff's tool who raced back. I swung with all my might. My balled fist whistled through air and clonked harmlessly against the house siding.

The bulking shadows of the police crowded all around. They cursed, stamped, swung wooden clubs and pistol butts. I danced into their midst, fists flying. One of the billies rapped me across the brow. That did it.

The world tilted and spun out of focus. Sheriff Peel himself blustered up, snatched a billy and bashed me again.

"This man's a mad dog!"

He was all wrong. I was just a very tired dog, about to be put on the end of a long, long leash. I slid toward the grass and blacked out.

# Chapter Thirteen

AT FIRST I THOUGHT we'd ignored August and September and I'd been mugged by a bunch of halloween goblins.

The swollen face hovering over mine like an image in a dusty lens had cheeks puffed out large as a frog's and a forehead that was a mass of angry wrinkles. A low-watt bulb with a tin shade straight out of a 1920 cops and robbers vehicle threw half the hideous visage into sharp white relief. It became even more hideous when I recognized it for the furious map of Sheriff Buster Peel.

Over his shoulder I glimpsed another party who seemed to be watching me with a frozen expression. I blinked, worked my jaw right and left. It still hinged properly. The second ogler was Coolidge under glass. From the cracked plaster and the cigarette smoke, I knew where I was. "Winnie! My God, Winnie!"

A hand thwacked my head. I subsided into the wooden chair set in the middle of the frowsy office. I groaned and tried to read the fine print on the bulb.

"Say, do we need that goddamn light shining in my face? It's pretty goddamn theatrical."

"We'll show you what's theatrical, Havoc."

Officer Simms had thumbs hooked in his Sam Browne and a scowl on his face that would have unnerved a Martian. A blood vessel in his throat was very active as he added through clenched teeth, "You smart little sonofabitch."

"Ahem! Watch your language there, Simms," said Peel. "No cussing at headquarters."

Simms steamed. "After what he did, you want me to— Sheriff, do you realize I've been in three practically fatal automobile wrecks? I also had my cookies crunched by

117

a bunch of old biddies who thought I was going to assault them. I made a horse's south end of myself running around Willoughby's Woods all afternoon, too."

I jumped up. "Listen, a girl's in trouble—!"

Simms threw out a boot which I didn't spot right away. I tumbled clavicle over shanks, hit my head on a bronze spittoon. I came up ready to punch. I pulled the blow at the last second as an eternally glum countenance inserted itself between my knucks and the quivering Simms.

"Now, now, Havoc, hold it!" He peeked down his long nose with his spaniel eyes. "Haven't you done enough already? Why compound it?"

"FitzHugh!" I seized his lapels. "Am I glad to see you!"

"Don't be," returned Detective First Grade Goodpasture sourly. "I came down as a personal favor to Buster. He phoned me three hours ago that he'd caught you."

*"Three hours? Is it that late?"*

"I couldn't resist driving in from my sister Hazel's. After all, this is a scene I've dreamed about for years. You inside a police station, finally brought to account." He sniffed. "Damn shame I couldn't manage it myself. Sorry, Buster, nothing personal."

"Make him sit down," said Peel. "I don't trust him on his feet."

"I'd like to put him on his ass, permanently," offered the cheerful Simms.

I protested: "But I tell you Winnie is being held prisoner by—"

Chomping on his weed and rolling his eyes heavenward, FitzHugh told Peel, "He hasn't changed a bit, Buster. He can invent more stories in five minutes than Scheherazade did in her entire married life. Frankly, I think Simms may have a point. Use the rubber hose now and ask questions later. You do have a rubber hose, don't you, Buster? We're not allowed in the city—that is, I assumed that here in the country—"

Peel contemplated his silent humorless visage. "There maybe some garden hose outside."

"No hose necessary, sir." Simms displayed his rugged right hand under the light. "Turn me loose with this and we'll soon have a confession." Simms folded my shirt several ways at once. "You rotten punk, do you have any idea what a hell of a job it is to clean peanut butter off a windshield?"

Peel waddled forward. "Now there, Simms! We have more important things to clear up than peanut butter on your windshield." He curled his lips at me. Despite the discussion of peanut butter, the cops were fighting mad. FitzHugh leaned back and worked his cigar, enjoying the spectacle immensely. Peel said, "Before we throw you in a cell we want to know why you killed Abel, not to mention Ham Anderson."

"Damn it, I didn't. It was those two hoods working for Bogardus."

Sheriff Peel elevated his eyebrows. "Whom did you say?"

"Banjo Bogardus! The heist expert who robbed the Rumsdale Iron Works fifteen years ago."

FitzHugh's expression grew a mite less skeptical. "I did hear he was out of the pen."

"You heard right. Not only out, but ensconced in Olympus Acres."

That strained Goodpasture's credulence. "See, Buster? He can't help himself."

I lammed both fists on the desk. "It's true. Banjo Bogardus is trying to dig up the loot from the robbery. It's buried under the basement of the Jones house at 72 Mohawk Trail. To make sure nobody interfered, he's holding Winnie prisoner."

"Let me get this straight," cooed FitzHugh. "There's a girl. Being held captive."

"In the basement at number 72 Mohawk Trail, right. Go and see for your—no! I take it back."

"I thought you would," he purred.

"But it's not because I made it up, dammit! Bogardus

said he'd hurt her the minute a copper stuck his face in the door. I believe him. He fried Abel and dumped Ham Anderson and he's dead serious about that dough whether you clowns believe me or not. By tomorrow night the whole crew will probably be gone."

FitzHugh made a fluttery gesture with his left hand. "Creeping away like Arabs folding their tents? Tell me, Johnny. How much assistance did the big bad man have in burying his money? Did the PTA help him? The Girl Scouts? Maybe all the Little Leaguers assembled and worked their tiny fingers to the bone for him." He sighed and scaled his worn weed into the spittoon. "Johnny, I really thought you'd confess with two murders on your conscience. I've always had you pegged for a shifty sort. But murder?" He shrugged.

"Buster, it's obvious, Havoc and Abel and that bartender concocted some scheme to swindle the local residents. Phony remodeling, bargain appliances. Something that wouldn't work in the city."

"I'll say it all night if necessary! Winnie Porter is being held prisoner in—"

"*Porter!*" Peel was barely coherent. "That crook! That swindler! What he did to those poor folks who bought his houses should have landed him behind bars for years. I had a hard time believing him when he said you broke into his place to rob him, even knowing you."

"Did he tell you—oh my God." I collapsed in the chair. "Then I might as well be talking to a bunch of Mongolians."

Irritated, FitzHugh snapped, "Come off it, Johnny. Admit you pulled a dirty caper and face the consequences like a man. Show some guts for a change!"

"I'll show some guts, you bunch of boobs!" I charged, letting my temper carry me to Buster Peel's paunch.

I gave him the right fist, then the left. I should have known better than to blow up. Officer Simms leaped to the fray. FitzHugh focused on the end of a new cigar while his friends lacerated me, dropped me aching and starry-eyed back into the chair.

I had to get out.

No matter what happened to me, I had to pull it out of the fire for the redhead who trusted me. And I had to do it alone.

They commenced the rapid-fire questioning again, Peel leading off.

"All right, Havoc. You employed one of your golf clubs to kill Abel."

"No, I throttled him with my purple Japanese kimono."

"Havoc, I warn you!"

"Warn me, warn me! Warn me to hell and back but at least collar Stan Porter and ask him whether his—oh, what's the use?"

Peel was disdainful. "It made me nauseous just asking him to sign a complaint against you, the low-life. I wouldn't touch him. Now what about Anderson? When did you kill him?"

I sighed. "Just before I took off to explore the Amazon."

"No more silly answers or I'll turn Simms loose!"

Simms tenderly massaged his knuckles. "Oh boy, do that."

I felt limp. "Silly questions, silly answers. All I want is for one person to walk in and be willing to listen."

"To a cheap hustler like you?" Peel unfastened his tie and really warmed up. "Judd Abel. Where did you meet him?"

"In the cockpit of a plane flying the mail to Denver."

"Goddamn— I ask you again, Havoc. *Where did you meet Judd Abel?*"

"I think Perle Mesta gave a party. We were swimming in this vat of champagne—"

"Keep after him," FitzHugh advised. "He'll run out of smart remarks in an hour or so."

I didn't, even though the answers grew worse and worse. With each new one I expected to be pulped into meat loaf by the snorting, cursing Simms or the snorting, cursing Peel or even by FitzHugh Goodpasture, who began to snort and curse himself as the dark hours of the night wore away.

Through a barred window overlooking the Sheriff's Department parking lot from one floor above I could survey the progress of the fat July moon. The more I tried to make them understand, the more FitzHugh kept referring to my past exploits.

Twelve o'clock came and went.

Two o'clock crept by.

The sheriff and his assistant were down to their T-shirts. They were wearing out the floor and consuming so many smokes I nearly strangled in the blue air. By four they were beginning to sag. But I wasn't encouraged, thinking of Winnie's plight.

I insisted my story about Bogardus was true. They insisted I was having opium dreams intended to conceal my guilt in some sort of racket which had backfired into double murder.

Around a quarter to five, the jokes got as stale as last year's crackers. Peel wiped his forehead with a bandana.

"Dunno. Just dunno. Never had a case like this. A liar who kept on lying."

The moon had set beyond the window. The spires of downtown Sylvan lay in the blue shadow. I felt like a phonograph: "The girl is in the basement; Winnie Porter."

Peel slipped into his shirt, knotted his tie, suppressed a yawn. "Let's go, FitzHugh. Gotta have coffee. There's an all night joint around the corner."

As Peel pushed his paunch through the door, FitzHugh climbed into his jacket and regarded me oddly. Peel instructed Simms to watch me with care, then complained, "Well, Fitz? What the hell's up?"

"Puzzles me. His attitude. I mean to say, Havoc's bad, right enough. Always involved in this or that seamy plot. But when he's run afoul of me before, it's never been worth more than sixty days. Somehow, listening to him field back those questions—"

FitzHugh yawned, covered it. "I must be tired. I'm almost tempted to believe him, nutty as his story sounds.

After all, Banjo Bogardus *was* released a while back. And the Rumsdale money was never found."

"Caffeine's what you need," said Peel with irritation. "Didn't you tell me the little crumb lies like a trooper?"

"Well, no, he doesn't precisely lie. He—ah—adjusts the truth. I want him behind bars as badly as you, Buster. But if a girl's in danger—"

"Hogwash!" Peel's voice boomed down the empty hall as they walked out. "Said so yourself."

"Yes, I suppose I did."

The final comment was Buster's. Supposing, to strain credibility, there was a shred of truth to what I said, did FitzHugh care to be the one to tap on the door of 72 Mohawk Trail at this hour? I wasn't able to hear the answer but I could guess it. Electric chair or not, the dice were all mine.

Officer Simms wore a leer that said he wished I'd get smart so he could exercise his ferocity. He turned briefly, latched the door. I decorated the back of his head with the plaster Cal Coolidge, frame and all.

For a moment Simms thought it was a gag. The obvious exit route was the hall leading past the switchboard where a man was constantly on duty. This fact made him hesitate a split second: "Why you damn silly little runt, you can't get out through the *roof*!"

I blasted his cast-iron belly, again, then twice more, polishing him off with a chair. I wedged him under the desk and rubbed my smarting knuckles.

Near the baseboard was an immense old-fashioned cold air return I'd spotted during the inquisition. It sucked draughts into the bowels of what I presumed to be a furnace in the basement. The grille of the return was nearly two feet in each dimension. I pried at the screws with a dime, hoping the air runs were as old and enlarged as the grille itself.

Taking a last look at the supine slumbering Simms, I jammed my tootsies into the hole, bent the rest of my abused self into a pretzel shape and dropped by inches down a vertical galvanized tunnel.

The drop wasn't rapid. Even at my miniature size, I scrapped the sides and lost patches of skin. Horrified, I glimpsed light below. Next thing I knew I'd dropped a few more feet and my map was plastered against another grille on the first floor.

I peered out at the switchboard as a burly officer was saying, "Yeah, Mrs. Shipple, right away. We'll bring a ladder to get the godda—to get your nice cat off the roof. Mrs. Wipple, do you mind my asking why your cat hadda go at four in the morning? This is our light shift. It may be a while before—yeah, I hear you, I hear you! What? Same to you!"

He pulled a plug from the board, mumbling darkly. I wiggled to propel myself further down the shaft. Then I realized what was hindering me—a circuitous bend in the return where it dipped below the lower floor on its way to the furnace.

Just before I squirmed around the bend out of sight, the desk man glanced up. His orbs contacted mine with the grille between. I kicked, shed more skin and finally tumbled into the horizontal pipe below the curve.

A funereal voice bellowed down the shaft, "Hello, is anybody—aw Jesus, I'm cracking up. Must be them candy bars with almonds so late at night."

He tramped back to his station, squeaking the ancient flooring overhead. My loafers came up against a meshed filter which blocked the end of the return before it entered the furnace.

I tapped the sides of the return. They clanged like anvils. Enough of that. Running my paws along the metal, I discovered a seam. Maybe another coin would help.

I lost two dimes, a nickel and a quarter in the dark before a half dollar finally opened the seam a crack. The sections of the air pipes were funneled one into another and held to the joists by loops of wire. After a series of hideous contortions I freed my arm up to the elbow. I worked on the nearest loop. Finally I released it and felt the return drop a foot. One section pulled out of the next, producing a small opening through which I could squeeze.

I hit the cement on all fours. The return sprang back its own accord, striking the other section jutting from the furnace with a fearsome whang. I crouched in the damp dark.

The voice of the desk man clamored down the shaft: "Say, Figby, is that you playing solitaire in the locker room? Figby? Oh hell, wait a minute, I'm coming. Cripes, where does everybody disappear to this time of night?"

His prattling about lockers encouraged me. I wedged open a pine door that went squee, found myself in a gray institutional hallway. A short distance away I discovered the empty locker room.

None of the tin items had locks. I selected the smallest uniform I could find, deposited my own rig under some towels in a laundry hamper. I took a final look at my disreputable mug as I splashed bracing cold water on it.

"Havoc, this had better work or even J. Edgar Hoover coming down from heaven on a ladder of gold won't help."

With the chin strap of the trooper's hat chafing my jawbone, I lowered my head and barged in the hall. Wouldn't you know, a couple of cops were just returning.

"Hiyah, Figby. Where you going so fast?"

"Signal ninety-six!" I bowled on hoping to hell there was one.

Might as well be hanged for sheep, I thought, whipping out the basement door into the parking lot. A prowl car was parked there. No, two. I chose the nearest, turned over the motor, cruised onto the main drag of Sylvan.

Passing a street lamp, I noticed light was winking off a dull blue-enamelled surface. I reached down. How about that! I'd managed to snatch a bullhorn. They probably didn't have many bullhorns in a town the size of this.

I stopped the bus and leaped out. Sure enough, small gold letters above the department emblem on the door said, *B. Peel*. Hanged for a sheep? Hell, I'd swing high in the name of the biggest ram around.

I leaned on the accelerator once I was clear of the village limits, heading for Olympus Acres.

# Chapter Fourteen

MY SLIGHTLY INSANE plan was predicated on two assumptions: One, even early on the Fourth of July dozens of souls would be whizzing along the freeway to beaches, parks and possible participation in auto insurance company statistics; Two, human nature hadn't changed since the pen of Harve Phiggs blotted paper.

The first assumption proved right as I shot beneath the orange steel undergirders of the freeway. Faint pearly light was mounting the eastern sky. The concrete strips overhead were already loaded with an unusually heavy conglomeration of autos barreling away from the city. The hum and whine of the wheels comforted me, if not exactly soothing my nerves.

The distance from the freeway to 72 Mohawk Trail by the shortest route, via petunia beds and back yards, I guessed to be a little over three blocks. I squinted into the dismal dawn as the silhouette of Castle Bogardus loomed ahead. Carefully I braked. The sheriff's radio began to squawk: "Attention all units, attention all units! Be on the lookout for Johnny Havoc, escapee from county jail."

There followed an unflattering description, a statement that the search was being personally directed from headquarters by Sheriff Peel, and an assertion that I was a mad dog. The airwaves crackled and spluttered with all sorts of rogers, overs and outs. I thought about hauling the mike from the hook to fake an answer until I tumbled to the fact that if Peel was manning a desk in Sylvan, he might not immediately notice that his own boat was gone. How long Buster would remain at ground zero I didn't know. An hour might do it, though.

The eastern horizon was reddening. I eased the police heap up the drive of the empty house across from the Jones' place. Already sweating enough to float the entire Cunard fleet, I circled the dump in the paling shadows. Leaning against the rear wall I found what I wanted— the tin *Open House* sign I'd seen before, together with some of those smaller markers real estate types erect on streetcorners to guide the unwary suckers into the trap. These red tin arrows on stakes I chucked into the prowl boat's back seat. Hefting the open house job, I ran across the street, sank the point of the stake into the loam of the Bogardus lawn. Before I sneaked back the way I'd come, I caught the steady racketa-racketa-racketa of an air drill chopping up concrete.

The drill sounded impatient. If they finished before I did—

I levered Peel's car into neutral, slid down the drive without a motor, coasted back along the street a few houses before starting the engine. I drove in reverse to the corner, cramped the wheel hard right. A minute later I parked at the curb in front of a familiar pad. The sun was beginning to gild the cheap shingles of the Home Buyer's Heaven on Earth as I thumbed the doorbell.

"Well for Crissake, this is some hour to be waking—"

Jinx Gordon goggled, scratching his paunch beneath livid chartreuse pajamas decorated with overflowing beer steins. He recognized me.

"Excuse *me*, officer. You're the guy who came over— Judy! Judy baby, wake up and make some coffee for the police!"

"No coffee, Gordon." I was growing more nervous in my impersonation every second.

He held the door open. "Want to come in? About that parking meter I knocked over after the lodge meeting?" His cheeks were persimmon. "The suds were really flowing. So was I. I'll be glad to pay for the damage."

"Skip the meter and pay attention. Still got your old army uniform handy?"

"Sure. Why didn't you say you were a sheriff's man the other night?"

"Official business. Confidential."

"Oh. Jeez, I'm sorry about that meter—"

"Stop worrying about the damned meter and do as I say. Round up your buddy Quinn, both of you in uniform. Be in your back yard in ten minutes and tell nobody. Oh, and collect a couple of those plastic rifles and machine guns I saw strewn around. There's serious trouble in the old Jones place." I clutched his arm. "This could have federal implications. Know what I mean? Just remember you're doing it for your friend Ned."

I started down the walk.

"Wait, officer! I'm no hero. Jeez, selling Hol-Dit-Furms you kind of soften up. I was in the old 44th Armored okay, but I sat on my ass in the company storeroom for three years."

"Gordon," I said, "they don't take kindly to damaged meters in Sylvan."

Old Jinx shivered uncomfortably. "Okay, okay. I'll be there. Alden too."

I changed the official heap around the block, coasted to a halt just beyond the driveway of 72 Mohawk, backed and parked the job diagonally across the street. No traffic could pass on either side. I left the lever in reverse, hauled the tin arrows from the back seat, locked all four doors so no helpful soul could move the boat. Hoping to heaven Bogardus and his finks were still occupied in the basement, I set off on the double through a nearby backyard. A housewife in pin curls, gazing out a kitchen window saw me and fainted.

I leaped hedges, jumped sandboxes, worked my way fast down the line in the direction of the freeway exit ramp, stopping only long enough to plant tin arrows at strategic spots on the parkway. Shoving the last arrow into the earth at the foot of the ramp, I said my prayers and started up.

At the top of the ramp a triple lane of traffic blazed by inches from me. Bumpers and hood ornaments caught

the sun. Several approaching cars slowed when I stepped
out on the concrete.

I jumped across to the center lane, wigwagging. I
stuck out my left arm to indicate the exit ramp.

It worked as beautifully as it had on the suckers at
Mammoth Cave.

Three cars turned off. One was a station wagon loaded
with shrieking moppets. The driver stopped, rolled down
the window.

"Officer, what's—" Horns behind squonked. "It's probably a Civil Defense exercise, Munster. Ask him if there's
a bathroom where we're going. Rodney is in agony."

Squinting from under the brim of the campaign hat,
I wigwagged my left arm sharply and said nothing. He
started up. Four other cars followed.

Behind on the freeway traffic was stacking up, fun-
neling into the right lane. Drivers leaned out, cussing and
pushing their horns. I kept signalling, sneaking a peek
over the rail now and then. The confused motorists
braked to study the tin signs, then followed the pointing
arrow. I counted forty-seven cars, waved the next drivers
straight ahead, ran like hell down the exit ramp.

Suburban doors popped open. Householders in disar-
ray rushed out to increase the tangle of flesh and auto-
mobiles backed up behind the roadblock I'd constructed
with Peel's vehicle. Naturally the confused crowd couldn't
stay inside the cars, which was all the better.

I cut around a house on the Jones side of the street.
A mob milled in front of 72 Mohawk. At the high hedge
separating Ned Jones' property from the others, I waved
to Quinn and Jinx, waiting in their uniforms.

"This way, quick! Bring those guns."

Loading my arms with Mattels and Ideals, I led the
way. Alden Quinn hitched up his horn rims.

"Say, what is this? Are we raiding a disorderly house?"

I blanched at the sight of so many men, women and
moppetts snuffling about on the Jones grass. From
houses in each direction, streams of people poured this
way. I ran for the boat, unlocked the door and dragged

out the bullhorn. I thrust the stupefied Sunday soldiers up close to one of the front window wells and ignored the swelling chorus of protests.

"Officer, Rodney here absolutely must find a bathroom."

"My God, don't just stand gawking, Newton, it's probably a Russian attack."

"Mommy, is this Pequamasspaw Picnic Grounds?"

I shoved a plastic rifle at Quinn, then one to Gordon.

"Hold it sort of parade-restish. Keep the butt on the ground." Switched on the bullhorn: "Attention Banjo Bogardus, attention Banjo Bogardus. The state militia is here. Come out with your hands up."

The air-hammer racket stopped inside. A second later a black window well fell open six inches. Who should be staring out, dark hair covered with cement dust and paw full of .45, but Banjo.

He turned white as the dust on his scalp just from seeing four khaki legs and some fake gun butts. The babble, though, sounded like a small army. He slammed the window shut. Jinx Gordon promptly fainted.

Doug poked his head out the front door, goggling, a rod in his fingers. In the house Bogardus screamed, "Christamighty, you fool, don't open—"

I hit the screen with my shoulder. Doug's gun hand still protruded through the opening. The aluminum door practically guillotined his wrist. The rod dropped into my waiting fingers.

With my free hand I hauled on his arm, tumbled him out to the stoop and gave him the butt over the head.

"Watch him, Quinn!"

I dove into the lion's den. Out of the basement rose piercing screams. Winnie's, no doubt of it. From the kitchen Lee Roy sprang out, lumpy face fierce, ready with his heater.

"Hold it, lunk." I showed him the muzzle of mine.

Bogardus blustered into the living room, followed by Zelda. She ran hands through her hair, sobbing: "Oh,

God, I oughta of gone into show business, I oughta of gone into show business for sure."

It was touch and go a second. Crouched and venomous, big Lee Roy couldn't make up his mind whether to turn the house into a shooting gallery. Bogardus settled the matter, clamped a pale hand on his hood's arm.

"Want to be massacred? Put it down." Lips twisted, he faced me. "You win the hand, punk. I won't tackle any army."

Lee Roy was trying to get a view out the front door. "Boss, that don't look like no army, that looks like—"

"Shut up and fetch Winnie Porter right away."

Steaming with hate, Bogardus hooked a thumb.

"Do it, Lee Roy."

"I heard you, I heard you." Sorrowfully Lee Roy passed me his cannon. In another couple of seconds, with this vicious crew out in the light of day, I could breathe easier. Bogardus handed over his own .45 without a murmur.

Lee Roy appeared again, pushing a disheveled but otherwise whole Winnie. She gasped.

"Johnny! How did you—oh, God, I thought they were going to kill me!"

"We would have, you dumb bitch," said Banjo, "if the midget hadn't turned out the goddamn state militia." He threw me a steely but grudging smile. "Punk, I hand it to you. What a partner you'd make. With your savvy and my muscle we could show them Chicago boys a thing or two."

"March," I said. "It's not brains, just hutzpah."

Zelda said: "What's that, a computer or something?"

"Gall, baby. Enough gall to be divided into several parts. That's right, Lee Roy, scratch the sky. After you, Banjo. Keep back, you people. These men are dangerous."

"Oh Jeez!" complained Lee Roy. "Look, Boss, women and kids and two guys in sojer suits."

Bogardus, however, rose to the occasion, shook his head appreciatively: "Why couldn't you have come from one of them bad environments midget? You're a criminal genuis."

"Thanks for the compliment, Banjo. Coming from you it's—"

"It's Johnny! Hiyah, Johnny!"

The pipsqueak voice belonged to none other than Junior Jones. He was attired in a bathrobe and was dragging his cane-propped father with him through the press. His big brown eyes glowed.

Doug had crawled to hands and knees on the grass under the gaze of a shaky Alden Quinn. At the sight of genuine cannons the crowd oohed, aahed and shrank back. Only Junior hurried forward with positively embarrassing adulation.

"See, pop, he's cornered the crooks who took our house, Johnny did it all by himself, he's a real—"

Junior's words were interrupted by sirens. I swung my head, saw with relief, if you can imagine that, the whirling red dome lights on a brace of sheriff's cars bumping to a stop at the fringe of the traffic jam. Buster Peel's corpulence lumbered along amongst the chrome. So old blubber finally tumbled to the theft of his—

Winnie screamed.

"Take that, Fink," Zelda cried, kicking me in a most unladylike place.

Banjo and Lee Roy needed no further signals. The former pasted me on the jaw, ripped the pair of guns from my belt as I fell and dropped the one in my hand. He tossed one to Doug. Next thing I knew, Lee Roy too had a fist around a heater, plus another around Junior Jones' midsection. The kid was howling and so were half the people.

"Anybody so much as exhales," Banjo shouted, "this little squirt gets a load of lead."

Lee Roy subdued the terrified Junior with a punch in the stomach. I leaped for him. Doug came up from the side of the stoop and caught me under the jaw with a blow of his cannon. I spun into a flower bed. The screams of the tourists were mounted.

"Run, goddamn it, and take the kid for cover!" Bogardus chopped the unhappy Zelda in the head. "So long, baby. I can't wait for a broad in high heels."

He leaped off the stoop as Lee Roy flung Junior over his shoulder. The deadly trio pelted toward the next lawn, menacing all and sundry with their cannons.

I disentangled myself from the flower bed and spat out a petunia. The hoods would use the guns, of that I was sure. Agonized, Ned Jones shouted, "Havoc, do something!"

"Arrest that man, arrest him!" bawled numbskull Peel down at the corner.

"Winnie!" I grabbed her trembling shoulder. "Hold those idiots off somehow. If Peel blunders after Bogardus, he'll shoot Junior."

She nodded weakly. The trio of burly boys vanished around a distant corner. I was plenty scared. People were fainting all over the place. I cut through a yard, then another, reaching the next street. Peel's bellow dwindled in the distance.

I ran until my lungs ached, catching sight of the hoods heading for a thick spread of trees at the edge of the housing development. Lee Roy carried Junior across his shoulder like a sack of grain. And I didn't even have a gun.

The streets of Olympus Acres seemed hideously empty. My lungs pained to beat hell. Bogardus and his mob ducked into the thick trees.

Suddenly I saw a string of expensive limousines heading down a curvy road that led into the foilage. From the black fenders of the first heap tiny pennons fluttered. The cars were moving a little faster than ten miles an hour. I covered the last block with my muscles aching, tore open the right door of the leading limo and punched the driver, a uniformed state trooper.

I kicked the brake, brought the limo to a stop, opened the other door and tossed the trooper to the pavement, retrieving his fat revolver just before he fell. A couple of outraged gents in the rear gabbled, "Officer, what in heaven's name are you doing?"

"Mister Mayor, is this the customary welcome Sylvan gives the lieutenant governor?"

"Thurston—your honor—I can't understand—"

I waved the cannon as I bowled the limo ahead, negotiating the curving road on two tires.

"Shut up, shut up both of you. There are three killers in the woods with a kid."

"Young man," cried the mayor, "those are not woods, that is the Olympus Acres Community Park the lieutenant governor was to dedicate later—"

"Yeah, yeah, I saw the sign. Shut *up!*"

I swung the wheel back and forth, peering through the trees for signs of life. Nothing, not a damned thing but sun dappling the ground, empty swings and merry-go-rounds and, across a big grassy field, huge cross-hatched wooden affairs on heavy pilings.

I was trying to figure out these items when a gun cracked.

The windshield shattered, showered my face with glass. The mayor had hysteria. The killers broke from a grove of elms near the road, Lee Roy in front with Junior still on his shoulder. Bogardus stopped to fire again.

Governor Sapinsley shouted, "Why, I believe that's—"

The crash of my gun silenced him. Bogardus ducked. His slug spanged off the limo's rear fender. The lieutenant governor let out a yell, dropped to the floorboards next to the mayor. Bogardus followed Lee Roy across the grassy field, Doug only a few steps behind.

The straw-haired young gunsel crouched, aimed and triggered. Only the fact that I was opening the car door saved me.

Glass blew apart in the window next to where I'd been sitting. Sharp shards rained on my neck as I dived along the asphalt road and pumped out a slug.

Doug arched, dropped his gun, clawed bark from an elm. He flopped in the grass, finished.

I crossed to the elms, peeked from the cover of a

trunk. I flung up the cannon for a shot at the retreating pair. But Bogardus was out of sight. I couldn't risk a bullet at Lee Roy. He was half-way to those screwy wooden frames, hauling the kid.

Where in hell was Banjo? In another minute I'd lose them.

The significance of the wooden frames penetrated.

Sweating hard, I clamped both hands around the gun butt, taking careful aim.

*Missed.*

The running hood would be in cover in a second—
*Shoot.*

I shot. This one went true.

With a whoosh and a roar Abraham Lincoln lit up.

His cheeks sputtered red. His beard and hair shot off blue stars. Lee Roy was frozen in his tracks, gawking.

I fired again. Sizzling started at the left of one of the biggest frames, zipped and crackled toward the right. There was the battleship Maine, going down in a sea of pinwheels.

Lee Roy flung up an arm to shield his face from the hellish glare of the fireworks. I blasted one more time. The slug set off Jim Bowie in purple, Davey Crockett and Colonel Travis in orange and *Remember the Alamo!* in pink letters of fire six feet high.

A concealed launching pad of Roman candles and skyrockets erupted. They whistled into the sky with a series of deafening reports. Lee Roy took one more look at that rain of fire, dropped Junior and fled.

"Hold it!" I bawled.

"Take him, Lee Roy!" a voice screamed. *"Crossfire!"*

There was Banjo, crawling from a clump of bushes, aiming at my guts, hate-faced. I took care of Lee Roy first, blasting him in the belly.

He lifted a foot off the ground. Bogardus shot. The lead gouged my ribs, knocked me flat.

Bogardus was up and running, bent on finishing me. He threw out his gun hand.

Trying to see through the fuzz somebody had wadded

in my eyesockets, I gave everything I had to one last pump of the trigger.

Banjo dropped his heater and capered. His nasty expression turned to a ghastly pallor. Blood seeped through his shirt fabric. He rolled over in the grass and lay still.

I heard a piping voice. Things were getting pretty thick. I managed to wedge an elbow beneath my bleeding rib cage and flop over on my belly. Junior Jones was stencilled against the melting fire, bathrobe flapping, tears in his eyes. Unless I'm mistaken there were a few in mine too, the relieved kind.

Junior knelt over me.

"Johnny, are you all right? Oh golly, you're bleeding something fierce." He looked toward the road. "Mister, over here! Hurry! Johnny, say something!"

I hurt too damned much to come up with anything very original. I read the most convenient message:

"Remember the Alamo."

Ten aerial bombs went off and I fainted.

# Chapter Fifteen

"Is THIS JUSTICE?" cried I. "Is this payment for valuable services rendered?"

"*Services?*" Buster Peel stomped around beneath the visage of Cool Cal.

After a full day sojourn in the Sylvan Emergency Clinic, during which time I found my flesh still intact except for some irritating packing in the wound a swathing of bandage, I was dragged by Peel's minions to his office. But with a little more courtesy than before.

The same vengeful crowd was back, however. Fitz-Hugh in his suit. Simms with a purple mouse under his left eye. Peel with his corporation quivering more violently than ever.

"What services? The trouble you caused with that trick on the freeway? The ruined fireworks? My stolen car?"

"Haven't you people got any mercy? My side aches like hell. I was almost killed."

"So was the Jones kid," he reminded me.

"You don't think I planned it, do you? Hey, how is Junior?"

FitzHugh coughed uncomfortably and masticated his moist cigar.

"Saw him this morning. The Rumsdale people came through with a handsome reward for Ned Jones. In the midst of all the hoorah over Jones buying back his former house, the little lad is pestering his father to buy him all the books he can find on Mammoth Cave."

"Mammoth—? That's my boy."

"That witless remark eludes me."

138

"I knew it would." All at once the scent of green arose. "What was that about a reward from Rumsdale?"

"Twenty percent. After all, Jones endured considerable travail on their behalf."

"What do you think *I* endured, a trip to Disneyland? Half of that money's mine."

"Where are you going to spend it?" inquired Simms. "The prison commissary?"

"Listen, I got the whole story from the doc. Doug was still alive when your people found him. I heard he and Zelda cleared me of both killings."

"Only technically," hedged Buster Peel.

"Technically I saved your technical bacon!" I exclaimed, leaping out of my chair. I upset the cup of coffee they'd brought me as a sop to conscience. Now it was a sop all over Simms pantaloons.

"You guys *laughed*! Laughed your heads off when I told you Bogardus had Winnie in—Good God, where is Winnie?"

"Home," said Peel officiously. "Resting up from the ordeal to which you subjected her."

"With her old man?"

"We have Stan Porter in custody as an accessory."

"Good enough. But you can't be serious about pressing charges against me."

Simms sponged coffee from his trousers. "Can't we?"

"It's time you learned," lectured FitzHugh, "that you cannot continue to make a mockery of justice and—"

The door crashed open. A type with silvery hair strode in, beaming.

"My boy, my *boy*! There you are! I made another special trip from the capital. Just to see you." He practically wrung my arm out of the socket. "Let me congratulate you. You were splendid."

"Splendid?" gargled Peel. "But your excellency! I mean, Mr. Sapinsley—"

"Gentlemen," said Lt. Governor Thurston Sapinsley, "do you happen to recall the name of the county prosecutor who convicted Emil Bogardus of the Rumsdale robbery? I see you don't. Well, my friends, it was none other than Thurston Sapinsley. It rankled me when I was unable to see the case fully closed and all the money returned. But *this* clever young man—ah, again I congratulate you, Mr. Havoc."

He did, mashing his fingers, his eyes loaded with official pride.

"You have removed a blot from the Sapinsley escutcheon. I feel heavily indebted to you. Are you up to lunch? My limousine is outside."

I grinned. "My pleasure, governor. Or is lieutenant correct?"

Sapinsley coughed discreetly, put his arm around my shoulder. "Elections next year, my boy. The governor is trying for the senate. Tell me. Have you ever managed a political campaign? Considering your superb skill at manipulating crowds—"

FitzHugh Goodpasture destroyed a perfectly good nickel cigar with his shoe as we marched out.

"How does he do it? My God, how does the little wretch *do* it? Buster, I—Buster, wake up! Buster—?"

"How do you feel?" Winnie wondered. "Really and truly?"

"Affluent." I kicked my loafers up on the coffee table. The sitting room was quiet.

"Affluent and ready to raise hell. Good old Jones. Good old trustworthy, honest Ned Jones. With fifty percent of twenty percent of that loot, I can pay a few bills, maybe even go whole hog and buy something expensive like a jug of shaving lotion. But who cares about finance? Come here."

She fended me teasingly, slipped to the opposite end of the couch.

"Johnny, you were only released from the hospital yesterday."

"Flesh wound," I said. "Speaking of flesh—"

I ogled the low bodice of the cocktail dress she'd donned for our dinner date.

"I can't see very well from here."

I hitched along the couch.

"Better."

She giggled, indicated the full brandy snifters on the cocktail table. Instead I tried a few tricks with my ten magic fingers. She giggled some more.

"Mr. Havoc, that's wicked."

"Shall I stop?"

"Want a punch in the nose?"

Her kiss made me feel like one of the set pieces I'd blown up in the park. The old house stayed quiet. Well, practically. There were noisy springs in the couch.

We never did get to dinner.

I think we had breakfast the next morning.

I'm *positive* we had dinner the following night, because what happened at dinner, with the wine, the candlelight and all—

I may become a suburbanite yet.

Also available from
The Armchair Detective Library

*The Shakeout* by Ken Follett
*Dead Cert* by Dick Francis
*Nerve* by Dick Francis
*Licence to Kill* by John Gardner
*The November Man* by Bill Granger
*The Blessing Way* by Tony Hillerman
*Johnny Havoc* by John Jakes
*The Big Bounce* by Elmore Leonard
*Hombre* by Elmore Leonard
*The Scarlatti Inheritance* by Robert Ludlum
*Cop Hater* by Ed McBain
*The Mugger* by Ed McBain
*Crocodile on the Sandbank* by Elizabeth Peters
*A Prospect of Vengeance* by Anthony Price

Collector Edition $25
Limited Edition $75
(100 copies, signed,and slipcased)
Postage & handling $3/book,
50¢ each additional

A trade edition with library binding is also available.
Please contact us for price and ordering information.

The Armchair Detective Library was created in affiliation with *The Armchair Detective* and The Mysterious Press with the aim of making available classic mystery and suspense fiction by the most respected authors in the field. Difficult to obtain in hardcover in the United States and often the first hardcover edition, the books in The Armchair Detective Library have been selected for their enduring significance.

For the production of these collector and limited editions, materials of the highest quality are used to provide a select audience with books that will prove as timeless as the stories themselves. The paper is 60–lb. acid free Glatfelter for longevity, bound in heavy duty Red Label Davey Boards, encased in Holliston Roxite "C" grade cloth and Smyth sewn for durability.

Printed and bound by Braun–Brumfield, Inc. of Ann Arbor, Michigan, U.S.A.